# SOAPSTONE

-by-

## John I. Carney

*John Carney 11/11/09*

*For Gail, Debra, Frank,*

*and all of my LEAMIS mission trip*

*teammates from 2003 on.*

ISBN: 1440451656

ISBN-13: 9781440451652

http://lakeneuron.com/soapstone

**ONE**
Melatonin Nightcap

Jeff Doerman shifted in his seat, dislodging the cord to his headphones in the process. He fumbled around under the blanket, found the end of the cord, and plugged it back into the armrest, restoring the soothing sounds of Norah Jones.

*I am*, he thought, *too fat to fly.*

Jeff went back and forth in his mind over whether to use the headphones at all. This was the transatlantic part of the flight, the part during which he was supposed to be sleeping. But he couldn't get to sleep. He had first tried turning everything off – no headphones, no seat-back TV, no solitaire on the PDA. But his mind raced. He had a thousand questions, a hundred worries, a dozen hopes.

*Am I up to this?*

He pulled out his journal – the blank book he'd purchased to record all his impressions of the trip – but he couldn't concentrate enough to write.

Teddy and Dea, sitting several rows ahead of him in the darkened cabin of the Airbus 330, kept telling him he was up to it. They were the organizers of this mission trip and eight before it – one every summer for the past six years, and a couple of shorter trips to Central America tucked in somewhere as well.

"Of course you're uncomfortable," Teddy had told Jeff during the pre-field training weekend. "A short-term mission trip takes you out of your comfort zone. That's part of the point."

But Jeff still wondered whether he'd be able to stomach the food, or get along with the people, or do without e-mail for two weeks while in Kenya.

Schuyler kept telling Jeff he was up to it. It was Schuyler, bless her heart, who had talked him into this in the first place, who introduced him to Teddy and Dea, who had showed him how to raise money. Schuyler, fast asleep on the aisle a vacant seat away from Jeff on the window, was a short, stout bundle of energy and sass. Jeff thought of her as roly-poly but would never have used that term in her presence; for all her bravado, he suspected she might be as sensitive about her weight as Jeff was.

She had known that Jeff would need to raise

every penny of his trip costs. She and her husband Rob – who was safely back home in the States – could probably have paid for Schuyler's trip all by themselves, but Teddy and Dea discouraged this, saying that fund-raising was a way of bringing people into the mission process. (Dea liked the word "process.")

In any case, Schuyler was able to spend some of her time helping Jeff raise money, and she carefully avoided asking any of their mutual friends for money so as not to take away from Jeff's support.

But then, Schuyler had looked after Jeff ever since they'd met at a church retreat a few years earlier. They lived in different counties, and didn't see each other that often, except at church-related events and a few occasions when Schuyler and Rob had invited Jeff over to their house for dinner. Jeff always wondered if he was supposed to reciprocate, but his apartment was small and he wasn't sure it was worth making Schuyler and Rob drive down for his meager hospitality.

"You just need a kick in the pants," she'd told him as they were driving together to to the pre-field training. "You don't believe in yourself."

"I'm 40, I live in an apartment, and I'm in a dead-end job. What's to believe in?"

"Cause and effect. You have to believe first."

"Whatever you say, Schuyler."

"You'd better listen to me. You may be a foot

taller, but I'm a dozen years older and fifty years wiser."

"Yes, ma'am."

"Don't be a smart-aleck."

Jeff looked over at the sleeping Schuyler and smiled. He wished he could join her. He had taken some melatonin, a supplement handed to him by a friend who worked at a health food store. It was supposed to help with jet lag when you travel east; you take the first dose at supper time on the day of departure, and then you take it at bedtime on your first few days in the new time zone.

It didn't seem to be helping over the North Atlantic.

Schuyler had taken some Tylenol PM, and had suggested that Jeff do the same. Now, he was wishing he'd done it.

He tried to get his hand on the armrest controls so that he could turn on the video screen, and check the progress of the flight. NWA, even in coach, offered the "map channel" on the seat-back video system, and Jeff, who'd never seen it before, was fascinated by it. He loved the way that it kept rotating between three different maps – a wide view that showed both North America and Europe, a closer continental view and a still-closer view with the names of small and unfamiliar places.

When he finally got the screen to work, he saw that the plane was passing over Greenland.

From Nashville to Nairobi, by way of Detroit and Amsterdam, hurtling over the chilly North Atlantic. What a world.

Jeff waited for the maps to cycle through, and then the statistics presented themselves – time to destination, wind speed, and even the sub-zero temperature outside the aircraft. He snuggled under his blanket.

He wasn't sure where the other three members of the team were sitting. Teddy and Dea had booked the tickets at three different times as the various team members turned in their air fare, afraid that the price would go up if they waited to book all the tickets. So the seats weren't next to each other. Jeff wanted a window seat, so he had gone online and moved his seat from the aisle to the window; Schuyler found out about this and moved hers to the aisle seat on the same row.

"So you can nag me the whole trip?" Jeff said.

"So I can make sure you don't try to jump out," said Schuyler.

As it happened, the only vacant seat on the aircraft was between them.

Kate Ackerman had probably gotten herself a window seat as well. She was fresh from college and hadn't flown a lot. Of course, there was not much to see out the window in the middle of the night over the North Atlantic, but it was the principle of the thing.

Jeff, unlike the willowy Kate, had another reason for choosing the window seat. He was overweight and sensitive about intruding on the space of the passenger next to him. From a window seat, he could lean towards the side of the aircraft and feel like he wasn't going to flop over and drool onto his neighbor in the middle of the night.

On this flight, mercifully, he had no immediate neighbor. But that still didn't help him get to sleep.

Axel McGuire was probably still awake, Jeff reasoned, because he couldn't hear Axel snoring over the sound of the jet engines. Jeff and Axel had roomed together during the pre-training weekend – and, as the two unaccompanied males on the team, would probably do so throughout their time in Kenya. For this reason, Jeff had brought earplugs.

He'd also brought Breathe Right strips. Jeff lived alone, and was overweight, and couldn't be 100 percent sure that he didn't snore himself. Maybe he did snore. Maybe he snored even more loudly than Axel.

No, that wasn't possible.

Axel and Jeff met for the first time at pre-field training, and went through the usual pleasantries of talking about their jobs and families.

"Get out."

"It's true! My name is Axel, and I'm a mechanic."

"Which came first – the name or the occupation?"

"Buddy, I've been Axel all my life, but I've only

worked on cars since I was 12."

When Axel first signed up for the trip, he had been under the impression that the team was going to Africa to build a church. After all, every other short-term mission team that Axel had heard about – and quite a few of them had slide shows at his church, to hear him tell it – had built a church in whatever country it was they were attempting to evangelize.

Axel made it all the way to the pre-field training with this idea lodged firmly in his brain. Teddy and Dea had to explain to Axel their ideas about partnership, and cottage industries, and economic empowerment.

"We're not going to build a church?"

"The place we're going already has a church," said Dea. "And if they needed a new one, it would be better if local people could get paid for building it."

"So, what are we doing? Are we preaching to them? Because I'm no preacher."

"You don't have to be a preacher," said Teddy, "although I might want you to stand up and give your testimony in church one night. No, most of the team is going to teach cottage industry workshops. Dea and I are going to make preparations for the classes we're teaching at the end of the week for the pastors in the area. And you are going to put in the water purification system. I've e-mailed you about it three times already."

"My wife checks the e-mail and prints it out for

me. Maybe she didn't print that one out."

Teddy and Dea looked at each other. Jeff caught a glimpse of it, and wasn't sure whether they were worried or amused by Axel.

"Axel's going to be fine," Schuyler had told Jeff later. "He'll be ready for the trip – or at least as ready as you *can* be for something like this. I think he's going back to Teddy and Dea's next weekend to work some more with the purifier."

Teddy and Dea had found a non-profit group in Indiana which manufactured a battery-powered chlorinator for use in remote areas of the Developing World. It used a car battery and common table salt to produce chlorine gas, which could be mixed with running water in a pipe or bubbled through standing water in a 50-gallon drum.

Schuyler's next door neighbor had recently installed a pool chlorinator which worked on the exact same principle.

"We're using this for swimming pools," sighed Dea, "and meanwhile millions of people are dying of dysentery."

"Think of it as an opportunity," Teddy had responded, cheerfully. "It used to take me five minutes to explain to people how this unit works. Now, some of the people we're asking to support us already know how it works."

"Hmm."

Jeff had not known Dea Concord very long, but

he already knew that she could pack volumes into a "Hmm."

Teddy, an accountant, and Dea, a high school English teacher, had founded Salt+Water Ministries six years earlier and ran it out of their home. They led a two-week trip every summer and had taken shorter trips once or twice during Christmas break, although the timing of the Christmas trips didn't work as well for Teddy and his clients.

Lucy Kemper, a real estate agent, was a client of Teddy's when he talked her on going on the Kenya trip. Jeff had been intrigued when he noticed Lucy reading Dave Barry during a break at the pre-field training weekend; up until that point, he hadn't realized she possessed a sense of humor. She always seemed worried – or at least preoccupied. Still, Jeff thought it might be worth getting to know her a little better. Every time he tried to strike up a conversation, she was just polite enough, for just long enough, and then suddenly remembered an urgent appointment elsewhere, and Jeff would watch the back of her shoulder-length brown hair as she walked away.

*My social life,* Jeff thought, *is even more depressing than my financial life, which is even more depressing than my work life.*

*But I'm not there right now. I'm on my way to Kenya.*

He squirmed some more in his seat and popped the headphones loose again. He plugged them back in, gave up on the idea of sleep, and turned the seat back TV to one of the movies. He wondered if it was really appropriate to watch a Jay-and-Silent-Bob movie while en route to a foreign mission field, but he shrugged and figured that no one cared, in the middle of the night over the chilly North Atlantic.

◆

As dawn broke, the Map Channel revealed that the plane was making its final approach to Schiphol Airport in Amsterdam. Jeff knew he hadn't slept as much as he needed to on the plane, but he figured he'd gotten a few winks. He might get a little more rest on the next eight-hour flight, from Amsterdam to Nairobi, although everyone had told him that sleeping on the transatlantic flight would be best for resetting his internal clock.

"Have you ever been to Europe?" he asked Schuyler.

"Years ago. I went to France one summer during college."

"I guess this will be my first time on foreign soil."

"And we'll be stuck in the airport for four hours," said Schuyler.

"I hate changing planes in a place that seems like it might be fun to visit. It's like adding insult to injury."

"Just as well," she laughed. "We don't want to show up in Nairobi smelling like ... something illegal."

"Is Amsterdam really like that?"

"I'm sure it's more like Sin City than where we come from – but probably less than the stereotype."

The plane landed and it seemed like forever for the plane to get to the terminal. At first, Jeff attributed this to his own anxiousness – the watched-pot-never-boils effect – but he finally decided that, yes, the runway was much farther from the terminal than at any American airport he could recall.

"Do we have to go through customs or anything here?"

"No. As long as we stay in the terminal, we're OK. We haven't actually entered the country as far as passports and visas are concerned. But we may have to go through security again before we get back on the plane."

Finally, after what seemed like an eternity, the plane was parked, the door was opened, and the people in coach stood around impatiently waiting for the people in first class to clear out. Jeff caught a glimpse of Lucy, a few rows ahead on the other side of the aircraft, reaching up to get her carry-on out of the overhead compartment. It nearly dropped onto her head, but she got control of it.

Jeff preferred to use his backpack as a carry-on and keep it stuffed under the seat, where he could get to it easily in flight. He slipped it on and edged closer to Schuyler so that he could stand up and get his head out from under the overhead.

"No rush," said Schuyler. "We'll be here a while."

"I just want to stretch my legs."

It seemed longer than it really was, but they trudged off the plane soon enough. Teddy and Dea were waiting for everyone at the gate.

"We've got four hours," said Teddy. "Let's move down to our departure gate and get settled there, and then if people want to wander we can do it in shifts and watch each other's carry-on luggage."

The departure gate for their KLM flight to Nairobi was on a different concourse, so they passed through a large section of the airport as they walked. There was a casino in the airport, and Jeff had to get a photo of it. There was also what looked like some sort of art museum.

"Where's the brothel?" Axel asked.

"That's an urban legend," Jeff answered. "I checked it out online after one of my co-workers started kidding me about it. Prostitution *is* legal here, and someone did seriously *propose* putting a brothel in the airport, but it got turned down."

"Oh, well," said Axel, and everyone within earshot laughed.

When they got to the departure gate, Teddy and Dea offered to watch the carry-ons so that people could stretch their legs, with the understanding that someone would eventually relieve them and let them do the same.

"We have to line up for security an hour before boarding time. I want to have a quick huddle before that, so we all need to be back here by 10:20 local time. It's 7:50 right now, which really only gives us about two and a half hours."

"Come on, Kate," said Lucy. "I want to go back and look at the jewelry we passed."

Schuyler was in the restroom, and Jeff didn't want to walk off without her, so he and Axel waited for her as Kate and Lucy scurried away. Jeff watched them disappear in the distance, the twenty-something and the – how old was Lucy? Jeff guessed she was in her late thirties.

Schuyler, Axel and Jeff made their way down the main concourse in a much more leisurely fashion.

"You guys hungry?" Axel asked.

"I am," said Schuyler.

"I could eat," said Jeff.

"Let's see what we can find."

What Axel found was ... McDonald's.

"You've *got* to be kidding," said Schuyler, horrified at the idea of flying to another continent and eating one's very first meal under the golden arches, but Axel thought it was funny and Schuyler begrudgingly agreed.

"At least it's breakfast," she said. "We're not having hamburgers."

"By this time two weeks from now, I bet a hamburger will sound pretty good," said Axel.

"I bet you're right," agreed Schuyler.

"I'm worried about the food in Kenya," said Jeff.

"I hope I don't, like, throw up, or offend someone by not cleaning my plate."

Dea was passionate about not wasting food and, during pre-field training, had stressed the importance of team members eating what was put before them. The people with whom they'd be working were poor, and couldn't afford to waste food themselves, she said. Salt+Water Ministries would help the team's hosts cover the cost of our food, but it would still be insensitive, and perhaps even offensive, for team members to leave too much on the plate.

Teddy, trying to reassure the team, had said that he and Dea were working with their hosts and would try to get the church and the host families to serve the team in such a way that team members could control their own portions. But he still said it was important for the team to accept the hospitality of the people in Kenya, and be seen accepting it.

"You'll be fine," Schuyler said. "Obsessing about it will only make it worse."

"One of my customers went on a mission trip to South America," said Axel, "and they served them guinea pig. I swear. Guinea pig. He said it tasted like squirrel."

"How did he know what squirrel tasted like?" asked Schuyler.

"What, you've never had squirrel stew?" Axel winked at Jeff, not because he was kidding – he wasn't – but because he was so pleased at Schuyler's reaction.

Jeff decided to move on. "So, this place we're going, it's right outside Nairobi, right?"

"It's outside Nairobi," said Schuyler. I don't know what that means – the outskirts, or a few miles out in the country, or what have you.

The McDonald's was located on an upper level of the main concourse, and Jeff looked down to see Kate and Lucy. They looked up and he waved at them.

"They weren't carrying any shopping bags," said Schuyler.

"They were just looking," said Jeff. "You're not going to buy jewelry on a mission trip. At least, not on the way out."

"And certainly not on the way home," said Schuyler. I haven't been to Africa, but I've been on mission trips before."

"What do you mean?"

"It's hard to explain. You'll know in two weeks."

◆

Jeff, Schuyler and Axel returned to the departure gate so that Teddy and Dea could wander for a while. But they discovered the team leaders dozing lightly in their seats. Jeff snapped a quick photo, and the group's laughter woke Teddy up. Finally, everyone was back at the gate – well before the appointed time.

"Let's go ahead and huddle up," said Teddy.

He handed out slips of paper for the team to use for reference when filling out their Kenyan immigration cards.

"This is Pastor Joe Mbuto's address in Nairobi," he said. "You want to put that down as our destination, since we don't know exactly where everyone will be staying. And like we told you on your visa application, the purpose of our trip is 'tourism.' That's just how they classify it, legally. If you put 'missionary' or 'missions' they might think you're coming for a long-term trip or what have you. It's simpler to just put 'tourism.'"

"But once we get past customs," said Dea, "I want you all to remember that you really are missionaries, not tourists."

"Exactly," said Teddy.

"By the way," said Dea, "for those of you sitting on the window, be sure and get a good look at the Sahara. I was talking to someone who's made this flight before, and they say it's really something to see from above. It goes on forever.

"If you're not in a window seat, try to get a look at it when you're up and about at some point. Sometimes there's a window you can get to at the back of the plane near the restroom."

"Very good," said Teddy. "Now, I think this is a good opportunity for prayer. Would someone like to lead us?"

No one volunteered immediately, but then Lucy broke the silence with a soft, "I will."

She prayed for the team's safety, for courage, for

focus on what they all had to accomplish in the days to come. She prayed for family members and difficult situations being left behind in the U.S. Then, softly, she said each team member's name, praying for each one individually.

Jeff felt the hair stand up on the back of his neck.

◆

The Sahara desert was every bit as incredible as Dea had indicated – an abstract painting in rust and amber, swirled out as far as the eye could see in every direction. There was no sense of scale – it could have been ten feet below or ten miles.

Jeff looked at the swirls and it made him think of soap.

Dea had asked Jeff to teach soapmaking as a cottage industry. It wasn't anything with which he was familiar, but he found a woman in the next county who made homemade soap and sold it at craft shows and in a few local gift shops. She was more than happy to teach him the basics of cold-process soapmaking.

After melted fat is mixed with a lye solution, and stirred for a long time, the mixture starts to thicken. When it gets thick enough, it can be poured into molds. It was the ripples and swirls on the surface of those molds that Jeff connected with the rippled sand dunes below.

When Jeff gave his first few bars of newly homemade soap to friends and family, he shaved off all the ripples so that the back of the bar would be as smooth and flat as the sides that had touched the mold. But he liked the look of the swirls and kept them on the bar he used for himself.

The soap needed to cure for several weeks before it could be used, and when Jeff looked at a calendar one day he realized that if he was going to take any samples of soap with him to Kenya, he needed to make all of them that week. So he made three batches of soap on three consecutive nights, using disposable plastic storage containers as molds. The plastic containers – meant to hold carrot sticks or some other small item in a lunch box -- were the perfect size and shape for a bar of soap, and Jeff was proud of his bars when he unmolded them all a few days later.

Jeff tried to nap a little more – he could never get totally to sleep, but felt as if he'd nodded off a few times.

The sunlight and the Sahara both disappeared as night fell over East Africa. Jeff filled out his immigration card with the information Teddy and Dea had handed out and his own passport information. He tucked it into the pocket of his backpack and checked the Map Channel for the tenth time in 15 minutes before trying to find a movie to distract him.

Eventually, the plane went into final approach, tray tables were returned to their upright and locked positions, and Jeff glanced over at Schuyler expectantly. She smiled at him.

The plane landed smoothly at Jomo Kenyatta International Airport, and Jeff's adventure had truly begun.

## TWO
Attack of the Wazungu

"Jambo!" exclaimed a cheery, round-faced man whom Jeff assumed was Pastor Joe Mbuto.

After the tedium of standing in line for immigration for a half hour and then standing around baggage claim for nearly an hour, the team had been waved through customs into the chaos that lay just beyond. Cab drivers looked for customers and other men offered to carry your bags, presumably in return for a tip.

Jeff was dying of thirst, but he wasn't sure if the snack bar would take U.S. dollars. ("Just about anyone at an airport, anywhere, takes U.S. dollars,"

Schuyler would tell him later.) He also wanted to see if there were any postcards; he had a sneaking suspicion that if he waited until the middle of the trip to send home postcards, he would make it home before the cards did.

But while the team had been waiting for its luggage, Teddy and Dea had tried to keep anyone from wandering too far afield. Now, they were presumably ready to leave, and so it looked like the soft drink and the post card would have to wait.

Teddy and Dea embraced Pastor Joe, and then and his wife Helen, who was standing with him.

"We have a van waiting for us, and I have brought my own car," said Joe. "Bring your luggage."

"And do not hand it to anyone," Helen added. While Joe's voice was warm and deep, Helen's was clipped and careful, but there was still a friendly twinkle in her eyes. Joe thought that their accents were almost musical, in the same way that a Cajun accent was musical.

Once outside the terminal, there was time for Teddy to introduce each member of the team to Joe and Helen. Jeff and Axel handed suitcases up to the driver of the rental van, who stacked some of them in a luggage rack on top and crammed more into the space behind the back seat.

Dea had given the team a speech about packing lightly. Her request had been only two small suitcases

– one for clothes and personal supplies, the other for workshop and other ministry supplies. Jeff had tried to follow this; some of the other members of the team has brought at least one big suitcase, and Lucy had two. Jeff thought he'd seen a look of annoyance in the driver's eyes at the huge pile of American luggage, but nothing was said and the driver did a skilled job of packing it all in.

Jeff, Lucy, Schuyler, Axel and Kate climbed into the van, while Teddy and Dea rode with the Mbutos.

It was dark out – too dark to take photos from a moving vehicle, Jeff figured -- but he peered through the windows to try to get his first look at Kenya. The area near the airport was peppered with the types of billboards you see around airports – airlines, banks and other business-oriented ads. There were also cell phone billboards.

"What time is it back home?" Schuyler asked.

"About three in the afternoon," Jeff responded.

Schuyler pulled a cell phone from her purse.

"You brought a phone, Schuyler?" asked Lucy. "Will it even work here?"

"I'm getting a signal," said Schuyler. "I checked with my carrier before I left the States to see if it would work. I'm just going to let Ron know we got here OK."

"I thought we were going to get someone to e-mail everybody back home," said Jeff.

"I know, but if I only stay on the phone a minute

or two, this won't be that expensive."

While Schuyler tried to get Ron on the phone to check in, Jeff returned his gaze to the street. He saw an American-style gas station and convenience store, or at least it looked that way from the outside. He saw numerous American-style businesses – seedy-looking, he thought, but not completely unfamiliar.

"What do you think, buddy?" asked Axel.

"I don't know. I'm still a little overwhelmed. Hard to know what to think yet. I guess I was expecting it to look like another planet or something."

"I know. I have buddy at the shop who thinks Africa is one big jungle. He figured we'd be sweating the whole trip."

"Not at this altitude," said Jeff. "We may be near the equator, but we're higher than Denver."

"Hasn't your buddy ever seen 'The Lion King'?" asked Lucy.

Schuyler's husband apparently wasn't at his desk at work, and she left a message for him telling him that everyone was OK.

Nairobi traffic was busy, Jeff noted, with cars, buses and vans bobbing and weaving (on the left side of the road – Kenya was once a British colony). There seemed to be few traffic lights; instead, the intersections of major streets seemed to be traffic circles. Jeff thought about the traffic circle near Music Row in Nashville; it had been built as a civic beautification project. But perhaps in a place like

Kenya, it was cheaper to have circles than stoplights. And they certainly didn't seem to slow anyone down.

"How are you doing back there, Kate?" asked Schuyler.

"I'm tired."

"We're all tired," said Schuyler. "Let's see; it's three in the afternoon back home on the day after we left. I got up at 5 a.m., so I've been up for 34 hours by this point except for tossing and turning on the plane."

"You were sleeping pretty well on the transatlantic flight, Schuyler."

"No one sleeps well in coach. I was lying still hoping I could get to sleep." She paused. "Wipe that smile off your face, Jeff. It's true!"

"Well, in any case I'll grant that we're all dog-tired."

"I can't wait to crawl into bed," said Axel. "We're supposed to do training tomorrow, right? I hope we don't start too early."

They pulled up to a security gate and the driver conversed with the guard in Swahili. Inside the gates was a smallish retreat center called St. Martin's. Pastor Joe's car had already arrived, and Joe and Helen and Teddy and Dea were already in the lobby checking the group in.

Dea stepped out to the sidewalk.

"When you get your keys, take your bags to your room and come back down here to the lobby."

"What for?" asked Axel. "I need to hit the hay."

"We're eating dinner."

"What?" This did not sit well with the group.

"It's apparently custom not to send guests to bed hungry. Dea had already made arrangements for St. Martin's to fix us dinner, and she even brought some fresh fruit and things herself."

"We're not really hungry," Jeff protested. "We ate on the plane. What we are is dog tired from the trip and the jet lag."

"I know, and I'm going to have to ask you to be flexible. Remember the training: flexibility is the key to short-term missions. We do not need to start this off on the wrong foot."

Eyes were rolled, but nothing more was said and the team filed into the lobby to get their room assignments and keys. The keys were old-style one-tooth skeleton keys, connected by a leather strap to a small wooden block in the shape of Africa bearing the room number. They were to be turned back in to the front desk any time we left the facility, said the desk clerk as each team member signed the register.

The staff of the St. Martin's was unfailingly polite and hospitable – a series of men appeared to carry luggage to rooms. Jeff, who usually tried to avoid situations where a tip might be expected, held onto his two checked bags, which seemed to puzzle the center's staff, and wore his backpack up to the room. Lucy and Kate let the staff carry their bags, but no one paused at the end of the process or gave any of the traditional U.S. signs of wanting a tip, so Lucy and Kate never offered one.

Everyone trudged back to the lobby and from there to the dining room.

After everyone was seated at the table, Helen came around with a pitcher of water, a bowl and a towel. She went around to each person at the table and poured warm water over their hands to wash them.

"We want to make you feel welcome here in Kenya," said Helen.

"I already washed mine," said Axel when Helen got to him. Helen moved on to Jeff, who suspected that perhaps Axel had done something wrong. Jeff held out his hands, and the warm water felt good.

"We wanted to introduce you to traditional Kenyan food," said Helen. "Teddy told me that you have tried to make some of these things back in America, but now you will see our way of making them."

The team had, in fact, looked up recipes for sukuma wiki and ugali online and had prepared them during the pre-field training weekend. But no one was sure if they tasted like they were supposed to, especially since the online recipes for sukuma wiki varied widely.

Sukuma wiki is a kale-based dish, usually with some other vegetables added in and a little bit of meat when it's available.

"For some of the people with whom we'll be working, it's not available very often," said Dea during the training.

Ugali, the great staple of Kenyan cooking, is a pasty white starch made from corn. To Jeff, a southerner, it looked for all the world like some grits that had been cooked too long and allowed to cool and set up.

Jeff had read in a book somewhere that the traditional way of eating in Kenya was to roll the ugali into a ball, form it into a little scoop, and use it to scoop up the sukuma wiki or whatever other dish you were eating. Jeff tried this, to Joe and Helen's great amusement. There was silverware on the table, after all.

Jeff could hear Lucy, who was right next to him, chuckle a little too, and he immediately turned red.

There were also some samosas, little savory fried meat pies which are actually Indian food but, Jeff would discover, have become quite common in Kenya, a cross-cultural remnant of the colonial days. The Kenyan version often contains beef, which would no doubt shock the Indians.

Chapati, a flatbread, was also served, as well as some of the fresh fruit that Helen had brought. The bananas were short and stubby, half the size of their American counterparts, but Jeff thought they tasted wonderful. He didn't quite care for the sukuma wiki.

The ugali was so bland that it was hard to feel much about it either way.

There was hot tea and coffee, but under the circumstances no one wanted caffeine. The kitchen staff produced some bottled waters, and after the staff had returned to the kitchen Dea checked to see if they were still factory-sealed.

"I want to teach you some Kiswahili," said Pastor Joe. "Habari za safari? It means, 'How was your journey?'"

"We haven't gone on safari," said Axel. "That's at the end of the trip."

"The word 'safari' in Kiswahili means any kind of journey, not just seeing the wild animals," said Joe.

"What is the difference between Kiswahili and Swahili?" asked Kate.

"Kiswahili is what Swahili is called in Swahili," said Helen.

"I cannot tell you how pleased we are to have you with us in Kenya," said Joe. "This is the first time that our church, Greater Vision Life Center, has hosted a team from abroad. The skills that you bring us are ones that our brothers and sisters need, and the water purifier will help us keep our people safe from cholera and typhoid.

"But even more than that, just your presence here as our brothers and sisters in Christ will be an encouragement. We expect large crowds at our church services each night, and we look forward to hearing what the Lord has placed on your hearts to share with us.

"Tomorrow afternoon, we will take you to downtown Nairobi to change money, and we will take you to see a bit of the city. Then, the next day, I understand that you will be busy here with training, but we may also take a short trip that Teddy and Dea have requested. Sunday morning, we will have services at church and then eat at the church afterward, and then you will move into your homes for the week.

"Now, I want to teach you a little more Swahili. Repeat after me: 'Bwana asifiwe.'"

"Bwana asifiwe!"

"That means 'Praise the Lord.' And we do praise the Lord for your safe arrival. But I know you must be tired, and so Helen and I will leave you to get some rest."

"Will you pray for us, Pastor Joe?" Teddy asked. Everyone stood and joined hands, and Joe prayed a prayer of thanks and blessing. He and Helen moved around the room and said good night to each person individually, which pleased Jeff.

After Joe and Helen had left, Dea called for attention.

"I think we will enjoy getting to know Joe and Helen during this time. Dea and I have been in contact with Joe for some time, but tonight was the first we have really gotten to speak with Helen. You may hear her called 'Mama Church.' It has to do with the way the term 'Mama' is used in Swahili. It's a term of respect for her as the matriarch of her congregation, and from what little I know of her I would say she's a very protective and good mother."

Teddy nodded. "I know it's been a long couple of days for everyone," he said. "I want to thank you for your patience in staying up for dinner tonight; it's important for us to honor the hospitality that our hosts show us, throughout the trip. The center here will have breakfast at eight in the morning. I know that's earlier that some of you would like, but we'll just have to deal with it. We'll have a short training session after that, and then, as Pastor Joe said, we'll go out into the city tomorrow afternoon.

"Now, go get some sleep."

Jeff didn't have to be told to get some sleep. He and Axel returned to their room and climbed into their beds.

Seconds later, they were dozing.

◆

Unfortunately, each of them assumed the other one had set some sort of alarm clock. Axel woke up at 8:30 Friday morning, awakened Jeff, and the two of them dressed quickly and rushed downstairs to grab breakfast.

"Can we meet back here in ten minutes?" asked Teddy after breakfast.

"Make it fifteen," said Jeff. "I assume the rest of

you showered this morning; Axel and I haven't
showered in a couple of days, and I can't speak for
myself, but Axel really needs one."

"Thanks, buddy. Same to you."

"We'll make it twenty," laughed Teddy. "I want
you each to wash thorougly."

The first order of business when everyone did
gather was to review the lists of items needed in each
workshop. Each workshop leader had brought along
some items, while a list of other items had been given
to Pastor Joe a week or two earlier for purchase in-
country. Jeff, for example, had brought stock pots,
molds and the like with him, but he couldn't take lye
on the aircraft and it wouldn't have made sense to
transport a large container of lard or some other fat.

Plus, as Dea had explained, it was important if
the cottage industries were to be maintained that the
church members learn where to find the needed
supplies.

Pastor Joe had given Teddy and Dea a report of
what he had been able to find.

"Jeff," said Teddy, "Pastor Joe told me he couldn't
find any lye."

"Oh, no!"

"Is that a problem?"

"Well, you can't make soap without it. That's
what soap is: lye plus fat."

"That's a problem, then."

Jeff thought a second. "How was it listed on the

list?"

"What do you mean?"

"Did you just put 'lye?'"

"I put whatever you sent me."

"Tell him to look for sodium hydroxide. Or ... what's the British term ...."

"There's a British term for it? Well, there's your problem right there. Kenya speaks the King's English."

"... caustic soda. Tell him to look for sodium hydroxide or caustic soda."

"Will do. He gave me his cell phone number, so I'll go to the front desk and call him while Dea's working with you on the next thing."

"What about the lard?"

"No lard, either – but you said beef tallow would be OK. Apparently, pork isn't as big here as in the U.S.," said Teddy. "Pigs have a bad reputation, I guess."

"Beef tallow will work fine."

Lucy's materials list for candle-making was fine, and Schuyler just needed plastic grocery bags, which the group had been led to believe were in great supply, for her crochet workshop. Kate had brought most of what she needed for the children's ministry. Teddy had already worked in advance with Pastor Joe to make sure that Axel would have the plastic drums, gravel and other supplies he needed for the water purification system.

While Teddy left the room to try to call Pastor Joe, Dea moved on to some material on cultural sensitivity, building on what the team had gotten during the training weekend back in the states.

"By the way," she said at one point, "don't forget that we're always missionaries. Can any of you tell me anything about your driver last night?"

The team members looked at each other silently.

"No one talked to him? Well, I know you were all tired, but that's kind of sad. Here's your first chance to interact with a Kenyan and you're staring out the window looking at the neon lights.

"I hope at least that you were aware of what you were saying. I hope there was nothing you said about Kenya that the driver wouldn't have wanted to hear.

"Also, Axel, I normally hate to single someone out like this but this is such an important point I want to make sure everyone hears it. The act of washing our hands before meal is not really about sanitation – it's a ritual. It's about hospitality. I don't care if a surgical scrub nurse has just washed your hands – if someone offers you that pitcher of warm water before a meal, you let them pour. Period.

"But I can't get on my high horse too much. I wasn't sure whether we were supposed to tip the conference center staff when we were checking in last night, and so I didn't. After all, I'm here to help these people, and I've got to watch our trip funds, and I didn't have shillings yet, and a dozen other excuses. I haven't talked to Pastor Joe about it yet, but I probably should have checked on what to do in advance."

After some more training, the team briefly discussed some of the skits that would be done during the worship services the team would lead.

"I am also going to call on some of you to give your testimonies," said Teddy, who had slipped back into the room. "Tonight, we're going to work on those. Each of us is going to share his or her testimony with the group.

"By the way – I have some postcards for everyone. Each person can have two. If you want to write these between now and this afternoon, we'll mail them while we're downtown."

The group broke for a light lunch, and then Pastor Joe and Helen showed up with another, larger, rental van. (This one had a different driver, Jeff noticed, and he wasn't sure whether he was relieved or disappointed at that.)

While the group was waiting in the lobby of St. Martin's, Jeff looked at some of the posters. The center was apparently owned by the Anglican church, and there was a photo of the local bishop hanging in the lobby and some diocesan newsletters on the coffee table. He also noted posters for an anti-AIDS initiative featuring the president of Kenya. The posters were beautifully photographed and designed, and the president looked both compassionate and authoritative.

"I and my administration pledge our most diligent efforts to the eradication of AIDS in Kenya," read the caption.

There was also what looked like a pay phone, and Jeff tried to make a call home to his sister in the U.S. using the instructions he'd gotten from the phone company back home, but he couldn't figure out how to get a dial tone. Apparently the phone wouldn't work without pre-paid cards.

It was just as well; Jeff thought about the time difference and realized his sister wouldn't be out of bed yet.

"Schuyler – did you get a hold of Rob last night?" he asked.

"No," she said, "but I left him a message. I may try again."

The team boarded the van and headed for downtown Nairobi. Helen pointed out the Jomo Kenyatta Conference Center, the city's signature building, and the van drove past the memorial at the site where terrorists bombed the U.S. Embassy in 1998. Twelve Americans were killed, Helen said, but over 200 Kenyans died in the explosion.

"We don't have time to go inside," said Joe. And there is a charge." The van drove on, and Jeff looked back at the memorial as the van turned a corner.

The van stopped on a downtown street and Joe indicated that everyone should get out.

"This is an exchange bureau," he said. "You can get shillings here for your dollars."

Teddy had made up laminated cars with the shilling-to-dollar exchange rate before the team had left the U.S.

"How much do you think we need?" Kate asked Teddy and Dea.

"I wouldn't change more than $200, and that's probably more than you need. Most of what you'll need shillings for will be buying souvenirs or gifts later on for the people who supported your trip, or maybe miscellaneous stuff during debrief. You shouldn't have to spend anything during the actual work week."

"We may stop at the Maasai market after church on Sunday," said Pastor Joe. "You can buy souvenirs there."

Jeff changed $200, stuffing the bills into his neck safe. The team re-boarded the van. While the team had been changing its money, Helen dropped off the team's postcards so that they could make their way back to the U.S.

Jeff had tried to write something cheery for each set of nieces and nephews, but there wasn't much to tell them yet. The postcards depicted Kenyan wildlife, and so Jeff wrote something about hoping to see lions and elephants during the debrief at the end of the trip, which would be held at a safari park. That would be impressive to the kids, even in the future tense.

"What are all the vans with the yellow stripe down the side?" Axel asked as the team left downtown.

"Those are matatus," said Pastor Joe. "Public transportation."

"Some of them look kind of rough."

"Some of them *are* rough."

Jeff noticed little kiosks selling Coca-Cola, and others labeled "Celtel" or "Safaricom." Joe said those were cellular telephone providers, selling pre-paid service.

"Are there many cell phones in Kenya?"

"All over Africa," said Joe. "Many people cannot afford telephone service, and the telephone lines may not go to all places. But cell phones here are simpler and less expensive than yours in the states, and people pay as they go."

The van made its way off the main road and wound around into what was obviously a poorer neighborhood, at least by Jeff's standards. Jeff noted that there was a different look to the neighborhood. Unlike the part of the city they'd seen last night, here there were old, weathered buildings. Many were painted from foundation to roof with various product logos. Some were familiar American brands; others weren't. Several buildings advertised an insecticide called Mortein Doom, and the phrase stuck in Jeff's mind. Mortein Doom. Mortein Doom. Mortein <u>Doom</u>.

Along the way, there were more and more people

walking on the roadside.

Then, the van turned down a side road and parked on a little bluff overlooking a valley.

Not much was said as the team walked out onto the hillside.

Stretched out before them, filling the valley below, were corrugated tin-roof sheds, packed together and stretching out as far as the eye could see in either direction.

"This is the Kibera slums," said Pastor Joe. "These are the people whom you will serve this week."

"How many people live here?" Dea asked.

"It depends on whom you ask. Some say 500,000, some say a million, some say two million. This slum is outside the city, and no one counts them."

Jeff lifted his camera. It seemed disrespectful, somehow, but he also knew he wanted to show this view the people who had helped to send him on the trip.

He wasn't sure it would mean anything. On film, he feared, it would just be a sort of man-made geology. He had trouble finding a camera angle that was wide enough to give you a sense of the size of it, but detailed enough to convey the essence of it, the vision of people backed in together this way, in these conditions. He looked at the display screen on the back of his camera and wondered if it was futile, continuing to shoot anyway.

Lucy also had her camera handy, and she, too,

was trying to capture the smoke and squalor – but then the children came running. They lived in a few of the sheds up on the hillside, on the edge of the slums, and they had noticed the presence of western visitors. They came closer and waved.

"HowaYOO," many of the children exclaimed.

Lucy let go of her camera and let it hang from her neck. "Can't do this," Jeff heard her mutter. He kept firing.

*I have to show people what this looks like,* he thought.

Lucy and Kate crouched down and spoke to the children. Several ran up to Axel, who still seemed staggered by it all.

"They can't get over seeing the mzungus," Teddy said to Joe, who laughed.

"What's a mzungu?" asekd Schuyler.

"A white person," said Joe. "It's Kiswahili. The plural is wazungu. It is descriptive, and there is no disrespect attached to it."

"I wasn't worried about it," said Schuyler. I just heard the word and wondered what it meant.

Jeff finally put his camera back in its case and stood, motionless, looking at the smoky sea of tin. Schuyler walked over to him.

"How are you doing, friend?"

"I don't know."

"That's a good answer, actually."

"Is this like what you saw in Mexico?"

"We didn't see anything on this scale where we

were, but Mexico's a pretty big country."

"How do people live like this?"

"I imagine we'll see how people live like this."

◆

After they left the bluff, they ventured back into Nairobi proper, but all the while they were winding their way through quiet side streets and busy thoroughfares around the edge of the slums, until they got to Joe and Helen's church, which was located right at the edge of the slums.

The church was surrounded by commercial buildings. It was set off the street a little ways, in a fenced-in compound behind a strange, solitary-looking building that was four or five stories high. It looked rough, almost bombed-out, and didn't seem to have any windows, as if construction had been stopped halfway through. It was surrounded by dirt and grime. Next door to the "office building," as Jeff thought of it, was a gas station, which looked sort of familiar, if dusty and unkempt. Nothing around either building was paved, although there was a concrete pad surrounding the gas pumps.

"This is a commercial area," said Pastor Joe. "Shops and businesses, such as they are, and stands selling various things. The part of the slums where people live starts a kilometre or so in that direction. But we will not have time to see that today. Later, we will break up into teams, and we will go and make some visits."

The Greater Vision Life Center itself was made of rough cinder block with a corrugated tin roof. There were wrought-iron gates over the windows, and shutters inside, but no glass.

Inside the church were plain, backless wooden benches, with a few high-backed kitchen table chairs along the front row.

A banner, hung up across the wall behind the pulpit, read "SPECIAL SERVICES JULY 5-10 WITH EVANGELISTS FROM THE U.S.A." Behind that hung a couple of brightly-colored knit blankets, perhaps to keep the sound from reflecting off the tin.

Facing the side of the church was a building with a row of small rooms which Pastor Joe said usually functioned as Sunday School classrooms. It was in those rooms that we would teach our cottage industry workshops.

Between the church building and the classrooms was a third, smaller building, which contained an office and another room. There five several boys, three of them young teenagers and the other two younger, standing in front of this one, along with a man in his 20s.

"This is Guy – he is my assistant pastor -- and these are our boys. We have taken them in here at the church, and they live here with us. This is John ... Paul ... Peter ... Mwai ... and Geoffrey."

The boys stepped forward and shook hands readily.

"It is good for you to be here," said one of the
older ones. "May God bless you."

Joe took Jeff and Lucy to the office to show them
the propane burners that the church had gotten for
the soap-making and candle-making workshops.
They were short, squat propane tanks with a little
burner "eye" resting right on top. Lucy and Jeff both
agreed that they would be quite suitable, and the
three of them walked back into the courtyard between
the three buildings.

Kate came up and whispered something to Lucy.
Lucy whispered back, and it apparently wasn't what
Kate wanted to hear. Kate then went and whispered
to Dea, who approached Helen. Helen took Kate
around to the other side of the church.

After Kate was out of earshot, Dea got the group's
attention.

"I guess we all need to know this. The outhouses
are over around on the other side of the church."

Helen returned and Joe talked with the group
about which room would be appropriate for which
workshop.

During this discussion, Kate showed up, looking
puzzled.

"Um ..."

"What is it, Kate?" asked Helen.

"Uh – where do you sit down? I looked in one
stall, and then I looked in the other stall, and – where
do you sit down?"

Teddy looked like he was about to laugh until Dea elbowed him in the ribs. Kate was as red as a home-grown tomato.

"Honey," said Dea, "I'm afraid you don't sit down. You have to squat. We're all going to have to squat."

"We will find something," said Helen.

"I know where we can get a stool designed for this," said Joe.

Kate gamely returned to the other side of the church.

Joe told the group about his plans to build an L-shaped second floor onto both the Sunday School building and church office. Axel beamed as Joe talked about how the water purification system would help benefit the community and avoid the risk of typhoid and dysentery from the wells or the other contaminated water that some of the people in the slums were forced to use.

When Kate returned – apparently none the worse for wear – Helen gathered the group.

"Please be careful of your valuables," she said. The group left the safety of the fenced compound and turned to an area behind the "office building."

This was some sort of little outdoor market. The stalls were made of gnarled, unfinished tree limbs, each maybe two inches in diameter, holding up blue plastic tarp.

The group entered the market from what seemed

to be the back, through a narrow gap between two rows of stalls. The ground was rutted, and filthy water was running through one of the ruts. There was a stench, and Jeff felt like he was going to be nauseous.

The market had a little bit of everything – some stalls sold clothing, some small household items, some soap and toiletries. The people working the stalls paid little attention to the wazungu, as if they knew that they didn't really have anything the Americans wanted.

Joe walked up beside Jeff.

"Look at the clothes," he said softly.

Jeff looked but couldn't tell what it was that Joe was trying to point out. Some of the T-shirts featured out-of-date movies and cartoon characters. There were T-shirts featuring the old name of an NFL franchise that had moved to a new city a year earlier.

In one stall, two men were ironing laundry. They used a cast-iron laundry iron which held a small amount of hot coals.

At the edge of the market, there was a Coca-Cola kiosk. Jeff looked at Teddy inquisitively and pointed at it. Teddy nodded, and Jeff went over to buy a Coke.

The price was 30 shillings, which, according to Jeff's laminated card, was less than 50 cents. But, given the average per capita income in Kenya and the no-doubt much lower per capita income here in the slums, Jeff thought it was amazing that anyone would buy the stuff.

To Jeff, though, it was delicious at any price.

After a good look around the market, the team headed back to the church compound.

"Did you notice the clothing?" Joe asked the group.

"What were we supposed to notice about it?" asked Lucy.

"When you give clothing away in the United States, to a thrift store or a charity, or when clothing goes out of style and no one will buy it anymore, some of it stays in the U.S. -- but some of it is sent here. That is generosity, no doubt, but it has also taken away our clothing industry. When I was a boy, my mother made and sold clothing. That industry was taken away when the cheap clothing arrived here.

"Nakumatt and the stores in downtown Nairobi sell new western-style clothing, and places like this sell used western-style clothing.

"No one sells Kenyan-style clothing anymore."

## THREE
Close to the Vest

"The point of these testimonies," said Dea, "is to share with others what God has done in your life. Tonight, I want you to feel safe. You may tell us more tonight than you're willing to say when it comes time to speak at the church in Kibera. In fact, what you say tonight may be quite a bit different from what you say in church. That's OK. But tonight is about telling our stories. Our Christian faith is a faith informed by stories. Jesus taught using stories. The apostles told their stories.

"Teddy and I have chosen our messages carefully, and I'd like to think that God will use them. But an individual, telling a first person story, can be a lot more effective than a preacher preaching a sermon."

"Actually," interrupted Teddy, "I chose my messages by throwing darts at a Bible."

"Thank you, darling. You can be quiet now. The point of this exercise is to help you learn to put your own story into words. As we get to know our hosts, I think you'll get a sense of what details of your life story will translate well from one culture into another, and that will help you decide what to leave in and what to take out when it comes time for you to actually speak in church.

"Now, in your preparation materials, we asked you to make notes about this, gave you some guidelines and asked you to bring your notes with you on the trip. Did everyone do that?"

Assent was nodded.

"Good. The one thing I do want you to start practicing is breaking your thoughts down into short sentences. Do you remember when we did that during the pre-field training? Even though many of the people we are dealing with speak English, not all of them do, and all of our services will be translated into Swahili. So you will have to learn to give the translator enough to work with – enough so that the translator understands where you're headed, which may make the difference in whether something is a verb or an adjective or a noun – but not so much that the translator forgets the end of the sentence before he gets there.

"This is a safe place. What is shared here stays here, unless the person who shares it here decides to share it elsewhere.

"My first instinct is to take volunteers, and I really ought to go first to model what I'm asking you to do. But I don't think I'm going to. Sometimes there's power in going first or going last, and since we're all going to be doing this, I think we're going to do it randomly. I have your names – our names – on slips of paper. Axel, will you pick one?"

Axel picked a paper and unfolded it.

"Kate."

Kate stuck out her lower lip and exhaled, making her bangs fly wildly. She got up and walked to the front of the conference room.

"My name is Kate Ackerman. I'm 24 years old. I graduated from college last fall, and I've been working for my father's office supply store.

"We always went to church, when I was growing up, and I guess I always believed in God. But when I was a freshman in high school, our youth group from church went to this retreat, and somehow the people at the camp made it real to me. I guess it's hard to explain. There were all these nice things people did for each other, and they had us give each other these affirmations – we were in a small group, and we had to tell each person what we loved and respected about them. And we sang these songs that weren't like what we sang at church."

She paused, thought, and then giggled, just a little.

"I guess it all sounds silly now, and I think it's probably because I'm doing a bad job of describing it. God was working on me at that camp, and I get warm fuzzies over some of the specific things about that camp week, but maybe it wasn't those things that changed me.

"Anyway, after that camp I got involved in this program where we went up into the mountains and worked on houses for poor people. That really touched me. It made me realize how lucky I am to have what I have, and a family that loves me and took care of me while I was growing up.

"I think God was teaching me that what I'm here for is to love other people and teach them about Him.

"And I guess that's it." She sat down.

"Thank you," said Dea. "Thank you for sharing yourself with us. Now ...." She handed the little pile of paper slips to Kate. "Pick the next victim – er, honored guest."

"Teddy."

He ambled up to the front.

"My name is Teddy Concord. When I was 19 years old, I wanted another drink so badly that I borrowed my college roommate's car and drove it to a liquor store. No one was at the liquor store, it being 3 a.m., and I threw a brick through the front window.

Having had other drinks, earlier in the evening, my peripheral vision was not what it should have been and I had failed to notice the police cruiser at a convenience store two doors down.

"A lot of college students get drunk. It's practically a rite of passage. But I found out very quickly that I was not like the other guys in my dorm. Once I got started, I couldn't stop. It wasn't a game to me anymore.

"I needed help. Fortunately, there were people who were able to cut through my 19-year-old bravado and get me help. Part of that help meant looking for something larger than myself to help give me the strength not to take the first drink, so that I wouldn't be tempted to take the second, and the third, and the tenth.

"I believe I know who that higher power is. I believe that the Bible is the book that higher power gave us, and the church, for all its flaws, is the way that we hold each other accountable for the way in which receive the incredible gift God has given us.

"But I am only a human being. I think there is such a thing as truth, and I have to be passionate about what I believe and try to share it with others. But I also have to be respectful of others who might be closer to the truth. People think the only two options are  self-righteous intolerance and live-and-let-live universalism, but I think there's a third way, and I'm trying to find what it is. I think an important part of it has to do with helping other people.

"Along the way, I met a beautiful woman who is my muse, my reason for living, my true soulmate. And if Dea ever finds out about her, I'm in big trouble."

"Stop!" Dea stood up amid the group's laughter. "That was very funny for our consumption, here in this room, but even though we realize we're talking to ourselves here, it's important to note that you do not want to use this kind of humor at the church. Humor does not always translate well from culture to culture, and if you aren't sure that the audience will know you are joking, you should play it safe. And you, of all people, should not be modeling this kind of behavior."

"You're right, of course." Teddy grinned. "But you shouldn't interrupt people while they're giving their testimonies."

"I wouldn't have interrupted anyone else. I knew you wouldn't mind."

"And I don't."

"Carry on, then."

"Dea and I founded Salt+Water seven years ago," said Teddy, pronouncing the "plus." Dea usually didn't pronounce it, and Jeff had thought it funny ever since the pre-field training that they couldn't work something like that out between them.

"We went on a few mission trips through our denomination, but we thought that in some ways they were missing the point. We wanted to do something different. And so here we are, in Nairobi."

Teddy reached for the slips of paper on the table. "Jeff."

"I've struggled with how to do this," Jeff started. "My story doesn't seem, well, doesn't seem all that inspiring. I don't have any dramatic ups or downs. I was a gifted child – an advantage which I've long since squandered – and when my parents had a conversion experience when I was seven or eight years old, I saw the change in them, and I wanted the same thing, and I tried to follow them a few years later. But while Jesus may suffer the nine-year-olds to come unto him, I'm not sure that a nine-year-old really knows what following Jesus is all about.

"I was kind of a loner in high school. Like you, Kate, I had some good experiences at church camps and retreats, but somehow I couldn't really turn it into anything back home, and I've always been awkward at making friends, platonic or otherwise.

"I went to Christian college, and it was, in some ways, the high point of my life. I had a network of peers, of people who shared a faith with me and who shared intellectually with me.

"I had big dreams when I left college, but I didn't find the kind of work I wanted and I ended up moving back to my little small town. And I was alone, and I wasn't accountable to anyone, and I managed my money really badly, and I got into debt, and I was feeling so beaten down by that whole process that after a while, I just gave up myself. I stopped even trying to ask anybody out. If I didn't believe I was worth being around, why would anyone else? I tend to be attracted to smart women, and I figured they were smart enough to know they could do better.

"But God never abandoned me. Even when I got discouraged – really discouraged – I could still feel him there, somewhere. And I re-adjusted my ideas of what success was all about and what the perfect life was all about.

"And then I started going to singles retreats and things like that, and it sort of re-captured a little bit of the feeling I'd had in church camp and at Christian college. I was at a prayer workshop one weekend in the mountains when I met Schuyler. And Schuyler has been my biggest fan ever since.

"I'm still lonely, and I'm still in debt, and I'm still frustrated with my job. I'm a white-collar worker at a factory. But, like Kate and Teddy, I think God is teaching me how to love people and I'm finding some sort of purpose in that. I started volunteering for a telephone crisis center and I work two nights a month.

"Sometimes I feel like I've wasted everything God has ever given me and I wonder how I'm ever going to get out of the hole. But God is in the hole just as surely as he's on the mountain."

And Jeff walked over to the pile of paper slips.

"Lucy."

"I'm Lucy Kemper, and I'm a real estate agent. A lot of people hear those words, and they think of someone loud, and brash, and pushy. I'm not loud, or brash, or pushy. When I'm working, when I'm dealing with sellers or buyers, I'm ... pro-active. I have the self-confidence you need to do a job like that. But sometimes I think that's not really me at all. I don't mean it's an act, per se, but it's not really central to who I am.

"I put a lot of myself into my work, and I take it seriously, and I'm good at it, but when I'm not working I think I tend to be very protective of myself. I crawl into a little hole.

"I'm telling you who I am. But that's not what I'm supposed to be doing, is it? I'm supposed to be telling you my story – how I got here.

"I guess I never expected God to find me. I grew up around people whose religion was loud, and self-righteous, and political, and seemed like it was completely fake and self-serving. My parents sent me to church camp, Kate, and to Christian college, Jeff, and I hated it. Hated, hated, hated it. I thought religion was a tool that people used to hit each other over the head.

"When I was 25, and single, I ran out of pills one month and I didn't have my copay and I took a stupid chance and I got pregnant. I decided to keep the baby, but I had ... I had a miscarriage."

"Even though I hadn't been planning for the child, probably wasn't emotionally ready for the child, I loved that idea of new life growing inside me. I wanted that life. I wanted to care for that life. I wanted to share the best of whatever was with that baby.

"I was working a cubicle job back then, and while I was pregnant one of my co-workers made me come to church with her one week because her son was being baptized.

"I wanted to be miserable – but this church wasn't anything like the church where I grew up. It was warm, and loving, and it was near a college and there were a lot of people who were literate and educated and I just fell head over heels for it.

"I think I wanted the community more than I cared about the truth. And when I had the miscarriage, and a handful of people from that church were so loving and supportive when I needed it, and challenging when I needed it, and I began to care more about the truth behind the caring. What made them that way? What was the difference between this church and the church I grew up in?

"And that's when I started to understand that I was right in the first place – religion is bad. But what I was seeing here wasn't a religion, it was a relationship. A relationship with God, and with each other, and with the Bible. And I grew into that. I don't think I had any one lightning moment of conversion; I just looked back one day and realized that God had brought me in.

"I wanted to be baptized, but in my denomination they won't baptize you a second time because they say that God's grace was effective the first time, whether you were in a position to receive it or not.

"I don't mean to turn this into theology, and I don't want to make it a comparison. Looking back, I think there were good and caring people in the church where I grew up, even though I know there were also a lot of people who weren't.

"I still don't think I've forgiven some of those people I grew up with." She took a deep breath.

"But you had it right, Jeff, when you said that God is good anyway. And that's the point; we're not perfect little figurines on a shelf. We hurt. We heal. And God is with us through it."

There were only three slips of paper left.

"Dea."

Jeff looked at Lucy while she was sitting down, for as long as he could look at her without being noticed. And he immediately second-guessed himself for doing so.

Dea, meanwhile, stood up and began to speak.

"For a while in college, I wanted to be a Buddhist. Lisa Simpson is a Buddhist, if you watch 'The Simpsons.' Richard Gere is a Buddhist. But when I was growing up thinking this, there was no Lisa

Simpson, and nobody had heard of Richard Gere. I just thought Buddhism sounded like an interesting way of looking at the world.

"I had just enough comparative religion class to make me dangerous. I never really studied Buddhism seriously; I just thought it sounded interesting.

"And I wanted to believe that all religions were different ways of talking about the same truth, different ways of expressing the collective subconscious.

"I was touring this Catholic cathedral for an art and aesthetics class I was taking, and I looked up and saw Jesus on the cross. That's a Catholic thing, of course; we Protestants have a cross, but we use it in a more abstract way. Here, in the Catholic church, I saw him hanging there. And I thought about Buddha, and I wondered what Mohammed looked like – of course, Islam prohibits you from that kind of representational art – and I looked back at Jesus there on the cross.

"And I said to myself, 'This is a relic. This is a symbol of a religious system that was responsible for the Spanish Inquisition, and the destruction of whole civilizations in the Americas, and this is just a hunk of metal.

"But somehow it wasn't a hunk of metal. Like you, Lucy, I had to struggle with the difference between the things that people do in Jesus' name and the reality of who Jesus is – or who Jesus was, since at that time I was thinking of him as just a historical figure. I looked at him, hanging there, bleeding and suffocating and pouring out his body and blood for the sins of the world.

"And it just made sense somehow. I couldn't process it right then, but it haunted me for about six months until I was able to start talking to someone from the a Christian group there on campus about it.

"I think it's funny that I found Jesus in a Catholic church, on the cross, and yet I didn't wind up as a Catholic, and now that I travel around the world I find that the cross isn't as widespread a symbol in some of these churches as it is in the states. I've been to many churches in the countries where Teddy and I have worked that don't have a cross up front at all; that seems strange to me, because I'm used to seeing either a symbolic cross or a representational crucifix. And yet, at this level, the symbolism doesn't seem as important as the reality. The people we've met on our trips are less about navel-gazing their faith and more about living it.

"We arrogantly think we're coming here to rescue these people. But I think we forget how much we're here to learn from these people. I think they've rescued me, and Teddy, more times than I can count."

Dea walked towards the two slips remaining on the table.

"Axel."

"I'm not sure I can tell my story as well as some of you have told yours. I got saved at a revival. I didn't want to come, but my wife talked me into it. She's always been good about coming to church, and brining the kids, and I guess we both thought it was important for the kids to be raised in church.

"But that's what I thought – church was something you were raised in. It was kind of like Santa Claus. Once you grew up, you didn't worry about it so much. You didn't really stop believing, you just didn't take it so serious.

"But Denise took it more serious than I did, and she came pretty regular, and she talked me into coming to this revival service. And the preacher talked about Jesus, and how we were all sinners, and how we all needed to be saved, and I felt it in my heart. I'm a Baptist, not a Methodist, but Teddy told me that John Wesley said he felt – how did it go?"

"My heart was strangely warmed," said Teddy.

"That's it. My heart was strangely warmed. It was just like John Wesley. And Jesus came into my heart and he changed me. And I don't want to watch the movies I used to watch, and I don't want to have a beer when I watch the game, and I want to go to Africa and help people – but not by building a church, right, Teddy?"

"Not by building a church, Axel. Not this trip."

"And I think I've been a better husband and a better father because of it. I hope I have been.

"And then I met Schuyler and Rob, and Schuyler talked me into doing this.

"Praise the Lord!"

Axel sat down.

"And ... speaking of Schuyler ..." Teddy grinned as he picked up the last remaining slip of paper.

"All right," said Schuyler. "Here goes nothing."

"Please," Dea said, "I don't want to hear anyone begin their testimony with 'here goes nothing.' Don't apologize for your story."

"I was 16 years old," Schuyler said, "when my 14-year-old brother died of leukemia."

A gasp indicated that this was new information to everyone in the room.

"He was so special to me ... he had red hair. His name was Gary.  He was learning to play the piano."

"Gary's death made me believe in God. Because that gave me someone to blame. I believed in God so that I could hate him."

Jeff felt a little ashamed for not knowing that much about his friend's past. But Schuyler had never mentioned it, never even hinted at it that Jeff could recall.

"I went through a dark period for 10 or 12 years. I wasn't anything like the person that you guys know today. I kept to myself, and I had a giant chip on my shoulder. I didn't start doing heroin, I didn't kill a man in Reno just to watch him die, I didn't need to check into rehab. But I wasn't really much of a human being.

"I know you're all expecting this big dramatic

story about how I started to see the silver lining in the cloud, but I don't really have one. I think I just got tired of it. I just decided that Gary" -- her voice broke -- "that Gary wouldn't want me to follow him.

"I met Rob, and that pulled me out of myself a bit, and I started volunteering for things.

"I woke up one morning in the early 80s and I saw a story on TV about people volunteering at the hospital helping to take care of the AIDS babies. They just needed people to hold them, to have some sort of contact with them. I went down there and I started helping hold the babies. Just hold them, and feed them, and sound like an idiot cooing at them.

"And it was just a process from there. Like those babies, I started growing up."

Everyone was quiet for what seemed like forever.

"Okay," said Dea.

"This has been quite different from what I expected. We've had some things shared tonight that will transfer into the African culture, and we've had some things that, I think we all understand, won't. But I think this has been a remarkably important night in terms of this trip. We were honest with each other – and I think that indicates how much we've grown to trust each other, through the pre-field training, and the process of getting here.

"I think we've seen here tonight that we are all growing and changing and reaching out. As we've told you, over and over and over again, short-term missions is all about flexibility. It's all about being willing to adapt and observe and change and cooperate. And that requires that we trust each other.

"Tonight showed me that we do trust each other, and I hope and believe that bodes well for our time in Kenya.

"Teddy is going to close us in prayer, and then I want you all to go and get some sleep."

## FOUR
<u>Let's Make A Deal</u>

Friday night, both Jeff and Axel remembered to set their alarm clocks.

"Buddy," said Axel as they crawled into their beds, "I thought I'd seen a lot of things, but the view from that hill today really got to me."

"Me too. And the market. Can you imagine standing under one of those sheds every day – or having to buy most of your stuff from one of those sheds?"

"What did you think of the boys?"

"The boys?"

"The orphans, at the church."

"Don't know what you mean."

"I just think it's sad that they live there at the church. I hope they take care of them OK."

"I'm sure they do, Axel."

"I want to try to talk to the orphans if I get the chance. Maybe I can get them to help me with the water system."

"Sounds like a good idea," said Jeff. "But, hey, we probably need to try to get some shuteye."

"I'll get the light."

◆

Saturday morning, Dea had asked the team to discuss their reactions to seeing the slums, the church and the market.

"... and the outhouses," laughed Axel.

Jeff decided he wouldn't have made such a joke without knowing Kate's feelings on the matter, but Kate seemed to be laughing at it. Good for her.

"And the outhouses," said Teddy. "Let's start with that. Was that difficult, Kate?"

"They smelled horrible," said Kate. And I looked, and there was nowhere to sit, and I wondered what I was supposed to do. I looked to see if there was some sort of hidden seat that flipped down or something like that."

"Also, did you remember to bring toilet paper with you like we told you two weeks ago?"

"Yes."

"Did anyone forget?"

Jeff held up his hand sheepishly.

"I got some extra back in the room," said Axel. "They make these little rolls for camping trips, in a little plastic case. You can put it in that backpack of yours."

"Good," said Dea, who turned her attention back to Kate. "Anyway, were you frustrated at the outhouse situation?"

"Absolutely I was frustrated."

"We will encounter frustration this week. Count on it. I have never been on a short-term trip where everything went according to plan, and there were no unpleasant surprises, and no challenges. I don't expect to ever go on such a trip.

"What matters is how we deal with the frustration. We need to find creative, positive ways of working through the frustration. We need to take the high road. If something is frustrating you, let someone know – not in a whining-and-complaining sort of way, but so that we can try to fix it. You may need to vent from time to time; that's absolutely OK, as long as you do it in a safe way, a way that's not going to offend our hosts. Remember, there's a fine line between getting something off your chest, which is good, and dwelling on it, which is part of the low road.

"As best I understand, we will have indoor plumbing in the homes where we will stay during the work week. But we will be at the church during the day, and that means using the outhouse. We're trying to deal with the seat problem, but we can't do much about the smell problem. If it bothers you that badly, come see me or Dea – we brought some Vicks Vap-O-Rub, and if you need to you can dab a little bit of it on your upper lip before you go somewhere that smell is going to be a problem."

Jeff raised his hand. "Actually, I can do a little bit about the smell problem."

"What do you mean?"

"Part of my soapmaking workshop will involve making sure that the students are very careful about washing up their utensils, because of the lye, which is dangerous. You can't throw your soapmaking stuff in with the regular food utensils.

"Anyway, I read on a soapmaking message board that you can pour lye water into an outhouse to help kill the smell. We can make sure they pour their wash water from the soapmaking into the outhouse, or if we need to we can mix up a little bit of lye water just to pour into the outhouse."

"Provided Joe is able to find the lye this morning."

"I'm trying not to think about that possibility," said Jeff.

"The fact is, any of us could find our plans disrupted. And if they are, we will just do the next thing. It's all about flexibility."

"Speaking of which," asked Schuyler, "have we gotten a good answer to the question about who's going to be in the workshops?"

"I think it's going to be the same people every day," said Teddy, "but Joe wouldn't commit to that. I think he's worried about what happens if we have a huge turnout and they need to rotate people through the workshops."

As Teddy and Dea explained it, the plan for Saturday afternoon was that the team would go to a produce market in downtown Nairobi and buy what they needed for that night's supper. If there was time, they might stop at the Maasai market, a place where authentic African craft items were sold.

The van arrived, with Joe, Helen and Oscar, another church member. Everyone clambered aboard and they headed for the produce market. Joe marveled at the traffic and at the abundance of various brightly-painted buses and the public transit matatus.

"I could never drive in this," said Jeff – who was seated far enough away from the driver not to worry about offending him. Vehicles dodged and darted as best they could, seeming to miss each other by mere centimeters as they brazenly pulled onto busy streets.

The market was a covered, partly-enclosed building at the edge of downtown. The van came to a stop but Teddy held his hand up before anyone got out.

"We'll break into groups," he said. "Joe will go with one group, Helen with one group and Oscar with one group. You can ask them about prices and what have you, but we want you to have the experience of buying what we need.

"Let's see ... Schuyler and I will go with Helen, Dea and Axel will go with Oscar, and Lucy, Jeff and Kate can go with Joe. Oscar's group can get vegetables and whatever else for a salad; Joe's group can figure out some sort of main dish – remember, we have no access to a kitchen -- and our group will get beverages and whatever else we think we need." He handed each of the other two teams an envelope with 300 shillings – less than $5.

Helen stood up and raised her hand for attention.

"You may see small children who ask you for money. I know that you are all generous, or you would not have come here. But I must ask you not to give them anything. They are professional beggars – working for a boss. This is a terrible system, and it is corrupt and bad for the children. We have rescued children from situations like this. Please do not support it.

"I know this is difficult – it is difficult for me, sometimes – but it is best for these children that you not support the way they live now."

"OK. Let's meet back here in, I don't know, half an hour," said Teddy. "No, make it 45 minutes. Have fun."

Jeff, Lucy and Kate huddled with Joe.

"A main dish?" Kate asked.

"Any suggestions, Pastor?" Jeff asked.

"Perhaps we should go and look first."

"Good idea," said Lucy. "Let's go look."

The produce market was a revelation. There were various stands with a cornucopia of different fruits and vegetables. Many of the fruits were luscious and appealing. Then, they passed stands with various types of meat – and while the area around the meat seemed clean enough, it looked strange and seemed somehow unsafe to see it sitting in the open.

"It sort of turns my stomach to see it like that," Kate whispered to Jeff when Joe was looking the other way.

There was rice in bulk, and there were beans in bulk – but that was of little use, without any way to cook them.

The three teams crossed each other's paths as they explored the market, each team wanting to get a good look at the whole range of offerings.

There were also some stands that had non-food items – soap and detergent and what have you. Jeff noted the soap was sold in bars as long as his forearm, scored so that it could be broken into individual bars.

"Pastor Joe."

"Yes, Jeff?"

"Are the people interested in learning how to make soap? Or is that something they'd rather just buy?"

"No, I think the soap workshop will be a great thing. Teddy and Dea spoke to me about which workshops to present, and I chose the soap workshop. I think if our people can learn to produce something like soap, that is a product they can sell.

"Oh – I was able to buy your sodium hydroxide this morning."

"I'm glad. Thank you for your efforts; I am sorry about the confusion."

"There is always a little confusion when people from different places come together."

Jeff had thought when he first met Pastor Joe that his speech and accent sounded richly African. Pastor Joe had playfully informed the team that Kenya spoke the King's English, not their corrupted American version. Jeff realized that part of what he had in his mind as "African" pronunciation was a careful, proud, precise pronunciation of English, a language which had no doubt been forced on Pastor Joe's ancestors by their colonial overlords.

"I hope I can teach the people of the church what they need to know in such a short time," Jeff said.

"I have no doubt you will do your best. The people of our church are excited to have the chance to learn."

There were some positions offering a small assortment of canned and processed foods.

"Canned food," said Lucy. "Maybe there's something there that we could get."

"Good thinking," said Jeff. Pastor Joe just smiled.

"Do you see anything like Spam?" asked Lucy.

"Not right away," said Kate.

"Maybe we could get some beans. Think of it as a meat substitute."

"Kind of bland," said Lucy, "especially if we're having them at room temperature."

"You've been to the United States, haven't you, Pastor Joe?" Jeff asked.

"I go about once a year to meet with the churches that support our ministry here."

Jeff picked up a bottle marked "tomato sauce."

"This looks like what we call 'ketchup' back in the U.S. Are you familiar with it?"

"Yes. Our tomato sauce is like your ketchup."

"Beans and ketchup," said Jeff. "Perfect. Of course, I'm sleeping in close quarters with Axel, and he's sleeping in close quarters with me. Maybe beans aren't such a good idea."

Lucy and Kate looked at each other and rolled their eyes.

"Let's get a couple of cans of beans," Lucy said, "and the ketchup, and take whatever money is left over and go back and get some of that fresh fruit."

"Sounds good."

The fresh fruit – oranges and avocados -- turned out to be 50 shillings more than they had left over.

"We're supposed to stay within our budget," said Jeff. "It's probably one of Teddy and Dea's training things. But I say what they don't know won't hurt them. You won't tell on us, will you, Pastor Joe?"

"My lips are sealed," said Joe.

"In that case," said Jeff, "I just thought of something else we need." He walked over to one of the stations that was selling household goods and bought a can opener.

"Nice catch," said Lucy.

On their way out of the market, Kate noticed a cart selling ice cream treats and the three of them used some of their personal money to buy ice cream sandwiches. Jeff asked Pastor Joe if he wanted one but he declined.

At the meeting place, they discovered that several other people had noticed the ice cream cart as well.

"What are we having for dinner?" asked Teddy.

"Beans and ketchup!" proclaimed Jeff.

"You have *got* to be kidding," said Schuyler.

"Sounds like a winner to me," said Axel.

◆

The Maasai market was held in a small grassy downtown lot surrounded by bustling city traffic.

There were various vendors selling crafts, but the individual vendors didn't really have much to do with selling their wares. Instead, as soon as the team arrived each member was immediately shadowed by at least one of what Jeff would later call, with some irony, "courtesy clerks."

Jeff's "clerk," who identified himself as Stephen,

followed Jeff around from station to station, peppering him with questions about where he came from.

"Oh, you are from the United States? Where in the United States? And where is Tennessee? Is it near Florida? What is your occupation?"

When not trying to make forced conversation, the clerk was constantly asking him what he thought about such-and-such an item.

Some of the items were beautiful and authentic-looking. Others seemed slightly cheesy-looking, like the little beaded key rings that said "Kenya." On a few of the items, Jeff half-expected to see the "MADE IN CHINA" sticker.

"These carvings are made of soapstone," Stephen said. "It is quarried in the western part of the country, the Kisii region, near Lake Victoria."

Jeff loved the little soapstone carvings of elephants and giraffes and lions. He picked up several of them.

If Jeff showed any interest in an item, it would be handed off to a carrier, with promises that Jeff could wait and pay for all of his purchases at once, at the end of the process. Questions about the price of an individual item would be diverted with promises that it would be cheaper to buy everything as a package. Andrew would then try to get Jeff to buy more of the same.

Jeff didn't like this system, and he didn't like the

way Stephen stayed so close to him and chatted him up in such an artificially-friendly manner.

*He needs to move to Tennessee and take up work as a used-car salesman*, thought Jeff.

When Jeff had finished looking at all of the items, he and Stephen walked away from the market onto a sidewalk nearby, where Stephen figured up a total cost for all of his items as the carrier called them off.

The total price, which Stephen quoted in dollars, was $85, about double what Jeff had expected and considerably more than he was ready to pay.

"I'm sorry. I can't," he said.

Stephen rolled his eyes in disgust. Alright. Eighty."

"No, I'm sorry for your trouble, but I think you just need to put all of that back. I... I got in over my head."

"What were you expecting to pay?"

Jeff was embarrassed to say that he'd only planned to pay $40, thinking that perhaps Stephen would be offended. He turned and started walking away.

"Fifty. Fifty dollars," said Stephen, sounding as if his heart were about to break and he were about to have to put his children onto the streets of Nairobi, all thanks to the cruelty of the rich American.

Jeff did a quick calculation and handed Stephen the equivalent of fifty in shillings. Stephen heaved a great sad sigh and handed Jeff his souvenirs.

When Jeff made his way back onto the van, he found Kate sitting there, by herself, in tears.

"What happened?"

"I wanted to buy one of those big elephants – the ones that were a foot high – for my parents. But the man was so pushy, and it was more than I could spend, and he just kept after me, and after me, and after me, and I just snapped and started crying."

"I was pretty close to that myself. I don't like this place, and I don't like these salespeople. It's not you; it's them."

Joe and Helen, who had at first been chatting with Oscar about some bit of church business, eventually figured out what was going on and injected themselves into the negotiations for the rest of the team members' purchases, conversing in some cases in heated Swahili rather than English. When everyone was back on the bus, Joe apologized profusely.

"This is not the market to which we normally bring visitors," he said. "That one is only open on Tuesdays, and so we brought you to this one, thinking it would be the same. But I see that they tried to cheat some of you.

"This is not the Kenya I wish to share with you. The market that is open on Tuesdays is quite a bit different."

◆

Teddy and Dea invited Joe, Helen and Oscar to

stay for the meal, but they said they had other preparations to make and simply dropped the team back off at St. Martin's.

The room temperature beans may have been an ingenious solution to a training exercise, but that didn't necessarily make them a popular supper in real life. Fortunately, the beverage / miscellaneous team had bought a small bottle of hot sauce, which proved more popular than expected.

The salad – which was based on shredded cabbage, because the salad team couldn't find any lettuce -- was refreshing, with a simple oil-and-vinegar dressing, and the oranges and avocados were wonderful. The avocado in particular had a much better flavor than the ones Jeff sometimes bought back home. Teddy and Dea had made sure the team washed all the produce in bottled water and not the retreat facility's tap water.

"What's on the schedule for tonight?" Schuyler asked, as the team was gathering up their dishes.

"Nothing," said Teddy. "I know everyone's tired from the trip, and the jet lag, and what we've done the past couple of days. And I know a couple of you may have stuff you need to do to prepare for your workshops. So we have nothing on the schedule tonight."

This announcement was universally well-received.

As they left the dining hall, Lucy turned to Jeff.

"I haven't seen any Coke machines anywhere except the airport," Lucy said. "I've seen those stands – what was the word you used?"

"Kiosks."

"Kiosks. I've seen those, but no Coke machines. I'd been hoping they would have some place to buy a Coke here."

"Maybe we could ask at the front desk."

"Good idea." They walked to the lobby; no one was at the front desk. They sat down at the coffee table.

"Well," Jeff asked, "how are you holding up?"

"I'm doing fine. I'm anxious to get started actually working. How about you?"

"I'm OK, too. The jet lag hasn't hit me yet, but I'm worried that it's just the adrenaline of being here, and I'm going to hit the wall eventually."

"You'll be fine," she said. Jeff wasn't sure if he was being patronized or encouraged.

"So how are things going for you back home? Business going OK, and all that?" he asked.

"I think so."

Just then Kate popped in.

"Lucy! There you are. I want to cut out some craft projects I'm going to be doing with the kids this week. Can you help?"

"Sure."

"Great! I've got it all set up back in the room."

Lucy turned to Jeff. "I'll talk to your later."

"Sure." The two of them scurried away.

Jeff stretched out on the leather couch in the lobby of St. Martin's and felt like the only human being left in the world.

A few minutes later, a well-dressed Kenyan woman appeared at the front desk.

"Is there something wrong with your room?" she asked, seeing him lying on the couch. He immediately sat up.

"No – er, no. I'm sorry. I was talking to someone here, and they – never mind." He stood. "I'll just be going now.

"On second thought – do you have any Coca-Cola?"

◆

Jeff was ambling down the corridor when he encountered Schuyler.

"Hey, Jeff. Whatcha doin'? And where'd you get the Coke?"

"Nothing, and the front desk. I was hoping they sold them, but they don't, but the clerk had one of her own. I'm not sure whether to drink it or take it down to Lucy – it was kind of her idea."

"I think you should drink it yourself, so that you can give me a sip."

Jeff grinned and handed the glass bottle to Lucy.

"Man, that's good," she said. "I've only been away three days and already I'm homesick for junk food."

"I'm the first-timer. I'm the one who's supposed to be homesick."

"And are you?"

"Not homesick exactly. Just ... ill at ease. Here I am, on the trip of a lifetime, not only doing God's work but getting to see all of these incredible sights, and other people paid for it, surrounded by team members who I love and trust, and I'm supposed to be a missionary, and as usual I'm sitting around feeling sorry for myself."

"Here. Have a Coke."

"Say ... that *is* good. You know, they ought to market this stuff."

"Your problem is you think too much."

"Agreed, but I can't seem to turn it off."

"You won't be thinking of yourself this week. I saw the look in your eyes when we were up on the bluff yesterday."

"You underestimate my talent for self-involvement."

"I also underestimated how thirsty I am. Gimme that Coke back."

"What if I want the Coke for myself?"

"You were going to give it to Lucy anyway."

"She didn't ask for it. It's more fun giving things to people who don't ask for them."

Schuyler placed her forefinger on the tip of Jeff's nose, and had to reach up to do it.

"You will learn, in the course of short-term

missions, that you aren't allowed to put restrictions on your generosity. Or it's not really generosity, is it?"

"I suppose not. Changing the subject – have you gotten a hold of Rob yet?"

"I didn't try tonight. It's Saturday afternoon back home – he's probably out playing golf or something. I'll try tomorrow night."

◆

Jeff found Axel stretched out on his bed reading the notebook with instructions about the water purification system.

"I was beginning to think you got lost, buddy."

"I was out on safari."

"Do you have any idea what church is going to be like tomorrow?"

"None whatsoever."

"It should be interesting. You ready for your soap-making?"

"I think I am. I hope what I have to teach is what they need to learn."

"It'll work out. God will take care of it."

"I hope so, Axel."

## FIVE
<u>Segregation</u>

The van, after another harrowing ride dodging the matatus, pulled up to the church fifteen minutes before what the team had been told was the scheduled service time.

No one was there but the orphans and Guy, the assistant pastor – not even Pastor Joe and Helen, yet. The team had checked out of St. Martin's, and so the van bore all of the team's luggage. It was unloaded and stored in one of the empty school classrooms during the service.

Axel was delighted at the chance to talk to the orphans, and they were happy to be around him but weren't quite sure what to make of him, and they were a bit shy about answering his questions.

"Do you have classes? Do you go to school?" Axel asked.

"Guy teaches us," said John.

"The little ones go to a school near here," said Guy, "but we cannot afford yet to send the older ones to school, so I try to give them some lessons here."

"Are you a good teacher?" asked Axel.

Guy seemed confused by the question. "I am not a teacher .... but I try to give them some lessons because we cannot afford to send the older ones to school."

Soon, people started wandering in. One or two team members commented on this, and Dea reminded them, privately, of the material they studied during their pre-field training about the difference between "monochronic" cultures and "polychronic" cultures, which place much less of an emphasis on punctuality or set start times.

Even so, when Joe and Helen arrived right before the announced service time they were apologetic, knowing that their American team members might well wonder what was going on.

"We had to stop at the store," said Pastor Joe.

Jeff tapped Lucy on the shoulder.

"You have to see this," he said. He took her around to where the two-stall outhouse stood.

The left stall door was padlocked shut and now

bore a sign.

"FOR OUR AMERICAN VISITORS ONLY," it read.

"We've taken a giant step backwards," Jeff said. "Welcome to the return of the whites-only toilet."

"That's horrible!"

"I know."

They quickly called Dea's attention to the sign.

"I didn't know about the sign, but I knew they were going to padlock the stall with the stool in it. Helen just gave me the key, so anyone who needs to use it needs to come find me."

"Aren't you going to make them take the sign down?" Jeff said.

"We aren't going to make them do anything," said Dea. "This makes us uncomfortable because we associate it with an embarrassing and shameful part of our past. But they mean it as a sign of hospitality. Now, what we want is partnership, not to be honored guests, but that's a process, not something we're going to achieve by stomping our feet.

"I told you yesterday that I want us to scatter ourselves out throughout the sanctuary during worship services. But for our first service this morning, they want us to sit up front as VIPs. We're going to do that – today. Then, we're going to try to act less like guests and more like family as the week goes on."

Music started emanating from the church; Dea,

Lucy and Jeff headed inside. There was a man playing a scuffed-looking electric guitar and another playing a modest electronic keyboard. Three songleaders up front led the congregation – what little there was, since many of the members were still milling about in the courtyard – in some sort of chorus.

The sound system was distorted, giving both the singers and the instrumentation a metallic sound, but the song – in Swahili – was one the church seemed to know well, and everyone was on their feet singing, some with hands raised. The team took their places standing in front of the high-backed chairs which formed the front row of the church.

The music was infectious, and moving. In one sense, it was like nothing Jeff had ever heard before, but yet the atmosphere it created was very much like the non-denominational charismatic church he'd attended once as a favor to a friend from work. It was strange, and beautiful, and Jeff wished he had thought to bring a tape recorder so that he could share it with friends and family back home. But it went on for what seemed to Jeff to be an awfully long time. He wanted to sit down. He looked up and down the row at his teammates and seemed to be alone in this assessment; everyone else was lost in the music.

Jeff noted how well-dressed everyone was. The team had to pack compactly, and for comfort. The American women all wore dresses, as they had been told during pre-field training, because Teddy and Dea were unsure about whether pants would offend local sensibilities. The men wore khakis (because they would air-dry faster than jeans, and because they would look better in church). Jeff and Teddy both wore polo shirts; Axel had on a new blue T-shirt. But the African men were all wearing suits and the women were all wearing fine-looking dresses.

Finally, the singers, and the congregation, sat down. Pastor Joe bounded to the little lectern that served as a pulpit. Oscar stood next to him and translated his words into Swahili.

"I will speak in English this morning for the benefit of our special guests," said Joe. "I will say one thing in Swahili: 'bwana asifiwe!'"

"We are blessed to have a team from Salt Water Ministries here this week from the United States," said Joe. "They will bless us with knowledge, and they will bless us with preaching and singing as well."

"Joe," interrupted Teddy, "I don't think we're doing any singing." He said it lightly, with a twinkle in his eye, but Jeff suspected he also seriously wanted to make sure Joe didn't overpromise what the team was going to do. The team and some of the congregation laughed immediately, and the rest laughed after Oscar finished translating.

*Does that mean only a third of them understand English?* Jeff wondered. *Or is it just a good idea to wait for the translation on things like humor?*

"Well, Teddy, we will do the singing, then. We know that you will bring a blessing to all of us. Also, on Friday, we will bring in pastors from throughout the area and Teddy and Dea will speak to them about ways to improve their ministry.

"Now, I would like for the team to introduce themselves so that we can know them all better."

The team stood and turned around to face the audience. They'd discussed this procedure with Teddy and Dea on Saturday; each team member introduced himself or herself and brought greetings from his home church.

As they stood up front, Jeff took the chance to look at the congregation. There were more women than men, and a good number of the women had children with them – *Kate should be happy to have this many kids to work with*, he thought. There seemed to be a range of ages.

After the introductions, Joe called for the offering to be taken. Dea had urged the team to always put something into the offering – it need not be much, but it would send a symbol. Jeff fumbled for some of his change from Sunday's shopping and placed it into the basket.

Dea then greeted the group and talked briefly about the purpose of Salt+Water Ministries, and about how and why she and Teddy had founded it. Teddy preached a sermon about fellowship and partnership, using Romans 12:4-5 and I Corinthians 12:4-6 as his primary texts.

After the service, team members tried to circulate as much as they could and shake hands and make conversation. But it was still early in the week, and Jeff found he wasn't quite sure what to say, and neither were most of the people with whom he spoke.

"Does it take a long time to travel from the United States?" asked one woman, who told Jeff her name was Grace.

"More than a day by airplane," said Jeff. But the conversation hung there; Jeff later decided that since the woman had obviously never traveled anywhere by air, her frame of reference would be traveling by bus, cross-country within Kenya – and it's possible that she'd been on a bus for that long, and so a 30-hour plane trip didn't really seem that impressive.

As the crowd dwindled, Teddy and Dea gathered the team in the room where the luggage was stored. He said the team would be staying in three homes.

"Lucy, Kate and Schuyler will stay with Joe and Helen," said Teddy. "Dea and I will stay with Oscar and Susan, and the gentlemen will stay with George and Elizabeth." George and Elizabeth had been two of the songleaders at the morning's worship.

"Oscar and Susan do not have a car, and so Joe is going to take Lucy, Kate and Schuyler home and then come back for Helen, Dea and me.

"Joe will have to make two trips like that for the week.

"All of your homes are in the city, not in the slums, and Joe assures me that everyone will be safe and comfortable. Unfortunately, because of the scheduling of this trip I haven't had a chance to see these homes. Dea or I should have found a way to slip out of training and go see the homes, but we couldn't arrange it, and that concerns me.

"If there's any sort of problem, just deal with it as best you can tonight and let Dea or me know first thing tomorrow. All of your homes will have bottled water, and they've been instructed not to wash produce in tap water or anything of that sort.

"We will have a team meeting first thing in the morning. Who's scheduled for our team devotion tomorrow?"

"I am," said Schuyler.

"Good. I'm looking forward to it. Since tomorrow is the first day, Dea and I will lead the meeting. Have fun getting to know your families this evening. Would someone like to lead us in prayer?"

Kate led a prayer for safety, fellowship and preparation, and each team member picked up his luggage and headed out into the courtyard.

George and Elizabeth had a beaten-up, weathered-looking car, but Jeff imagined that still placed them far ahead of their countrymen, most of whom seemed to either walk or ride the weather-beaten, yellow-striped matatus.

George, who was young and energetic, worked as

a bank teller, while Elizabeth worked in an office in downtown Nairobi. They had helped Joe and Helen found Greater Vision Life Center three years earlier. Their daughter Sally appeared to be about five years old. She was shy, and hid behind her mother when Axel tried to talk to her.

They climbed into the car. Jeff sat up front, with George, while Axel, Elizabeth and Sally sat in the back seat. Child safety seats apparently weren't required in Kenya, Jeff noticed.

"There are too many people here in Nairobi who want to ignore the slums," said George. "I know people who want to pretend that Nairobi is ... No. I know people who think that the most important thing in the world is for Nairobi to become a great city of business. When that happens, it will help all of the people of Kenya. But the people of slums are here, right now, and they need our attention. Pastor Joe sees this. Mama Church sees this.

"Pastor Joe is excited about the vision that you bring for the cottage industries. Anything we can do to help the people of the slums make something for themselves, make something of themselves, is a step forward."

They passed back into town.

"We hope you will be comfortable at our home," said Elizabeth. "We are so glad that you have come to Kenya to work with us."

"Are you hungry?" George asked.

"I am," responded Axel.

"We will go to Steers."

Steers, it turned out, was an American-style fast food restaurant chain.

"We thought you would enjoy this," said Elizabeth.

"Thank you very much," said Jeff. "We appreciate your hospitality."

Axel had a hamburger, which he proclaimed to be quite good, while Jeff tried the fried chicken. It was relatively good, although the pieces were somewhat smaller than Jeff was expecting.

Sally munched happily on fries, although she continued to resist Axel's attempts to make friends.

After the meal, they wound their way into a residential neighborhood. Jeff noted the little shops and kiosks on the side street, and more of the shabby-looking buildings painted with various logos and advertising slogans. Then the car pulled up to a gate with a man standing next to it. He came over, recognized George, and opened a large metal gate to let the car in to a side street. As they pulled in, Jeff realized that this was a gated community – gated for security, like a high-end subdivision back in the U.S., but gritty and shabby-looking.

Even within the gated area, the townhouse-like buildings had high, wall-like fences separating one lot from the other and shutting the homes off from the street. Some had broken glass protruding from the top of the fences, while others had razor wire.

They pulled up to George and Elizabeth's townhouse and parked on the street. There was a large gate with a smaller door cut into it. George unlocked the door and they walked in. Behind the gate was a small driveway, but George kept the car out on the street during the day.

The townhouse was rather western-looking, although modest – not at all what Jeff had been expecting. Jeff and Axel would sleep on cots in a small room on the first floor of the townhouse. There was a bathroom downstairs. It looked much rougher than the rest of the house and had an unusual-looking shower head. Jeff called Axel into the bathroom and pointed it out to him.

"It doesn't use a water heater," Axel explained to Jeff. "They may not even have a water heater. This shower head heats the water as it passes through. It's called a 'widowmaker' because the ones they used to make generations ago were a little dangerous."

He had a little twinkle in his eye as he caught Jeff's glance. "But I'm sure this one's fine."

There was a blue plastic 50-gallon drum sitting next to the shower stall.

"I wonder if they have many outages," Jeff mused, "or if they're saving grey water, or what."

"One thing's for sure, buddy – we're gonna send the wrong impression if we hang out in the bathroom together."

"Good point," said Jeff, laughing. They left the bathroom and wandered around the corner into the cramped living room, which apparently also served as the dining room, having a table and chairs at one end. George was upstairs and Elizabeth had gone to retrieve Sally.

"Wanna see what's on TV?" asked Jeff.

Axel found a remote control and turned on the television.

They were amused to see "Sanford and Son," and there was quickly a promo for "Diff'rent Strokes" to follow.

Jeff looked at Axel.

"No wonder the rest of the world hates us."

"I *like* 'Sanford and Son.'"

They heard someone coming in the door and Jeff snapped off the TV.

Elizabeth and Sally entered.

"Hi there, little one," said Axel, but Sally darted behind her mother.

"Wait right here," said Jeff. He bolted for his room and came back with a handful of individually-wrapped Life Savers.

"Is it all right if Sally has a piece of candy?"

Elizabeth smiled and nodded. Jeff unwrapped one of the Life Savers and handed it to Sally. Sally took it, tried it, and liked it.

"I think you made a friend, buddy."

"She is a beautiful child," said Jeff.

Elizabeth laughed at the expression on her daughter's face, then turned back to Axel and Jeff.

"Is your room all right? Do you have everything you need?"

"It's exactly what we need," said Jeff.

"If you have laundry, you can give it to me at breakfast tomorrow morning."

"If you show me where the machine is," said Axel, "I can do it myself."

"Machine?" asked Elizabeth, somewhat confused.

"The washing machine."

"We do not have a washing machine," Elizabeth said. "There is a girl from the neighborhood who comes and takes the washing. She does it by hand."

"That will be fine," said Jeff. "We don't want to be any inconvenience."

"Would you like conflicts in the morning?" Elizabeth asked.

"Pardon me?" asked Jeff.

"Would you like conflicts in the morning?"

Jeff and Axel looked at each other and shrugged.

"I'm not sure I know what you mean," said Jeff.

Elizabeth went into the kitchen and came back out with a box of ... corn flakes.

"Oh, corn flakes!" said Axel. "That would be great. We'd love corn flakes in the morning."

George came back downstairs and the four of them sat in the living room, while Sally was up in her room playing.

"So ... " Jeff wasn't quite sure what to say.

"What do you do back in the United States?" George asked. "Are you pastors?"

"No," said Jeff. "I work in quality control record-keeping at a factory that makes pencils."

"Quality control."

"I keep records about how many pencils come through the line in perfect condition, so that we can sell them, and how many are damaged or flawed, and we can't sell them, or we have to sell them as factory seconds. And we study ways to improve our process so that we produce more of the perfect pencils and fewer of the bad pencils."

*He's not an idiot*, Jeff told himself. *He's a bank teller. I don't need to talk to him like a third grader.*

"I work as an auto mechanic," said Axel. "I fix cars."

"I wish you had been here last week," laughed George.

They sat silently for a few more seconds.

"Would you like to watch the television?" asked Elizabeth.

"No," said Jeff. He was lying; he figured the TV would be preferable to sitting around awkwardly, but he also figured it would be rude.

"I'll be right back," said Axel. He disappeared to his room and came back with a game.

"Have you ever played Jenga?" he asked.

"No," said George. "Did you buy that here in

Kenya?"

"No. I brought it with me from the states."

"From the states – then why is it in Kiswahili?"

"It's not."

"'Jenga' is the Swahili word for 'build,'" said George.

"If that don't beat all," said Axel. "They must have done that on purpose."

Axel slid the tower of wooden blocks carefully out of the box and onto the coffee table.

"You can only use one hand," said Axel. "You can touch the blocks to see which ones are loose and which ones aren't, but you can only use one hand. You take a block from the middle of the tower and put it on top. You don't want to knock over the tower."

Axel moved a block and then gestured to Elizabeth, who tried her hand. George was next, and then Jeff. Elizabeth was delighted by the game and George seemed pleased by it as well, although he wasn't as expressive about it. Eventually, of course, the tower was knocked over – by Jeff – and everyone squealed with delight. The noise attracted Sally's attention, and she tromped downstairs in time to see the tower being rebuilt.

"I want to play!" she squealed, the first words she'd spoken in Jeff and Axel's presence since they'd all arrived home.

Jeff and Axel wanted to let her, but George and

Elizabeth were intent upon another game and made her keep hands off.

After a second game, George, who had appeared deep in thought, asked a question.

"How do you win?"

"What?"

"How do you win the game?"

Axel and Jeff looked at each other.

"Well, you lose the game by knocking over the tower."

"Yes, but how do you win?"

"I don't know," said Jeff. "I guess you could keep track of who knocks the tower over, and the last person who hasn't knocked it over is the winner."

"That is a strange way to win."

"I guess it is," said Jeff. "I haven't really thought about it before."

"It's just a fun game," said Elizabeth. "You take it too seriously, George."

"I think Sally should get a chance to play," said Axel. He set up the tower. They played a game with Sally, and when she knocked over the tower she was both disappointed and delighted.

Elizabeth went to the kitchen to prepare dinner – small sausages and rice. After dinner, they watched a local Nairobi newscast, which was followed by world news from the BBC, and then as Elizabeth put Sally to bed the men watched "CSI."

Jeff was a little uncomfortable watching the crime

drama.

"Do you think that this is what America is like?" he asked.

"What do you mean?" said George.

"People shooting each other all the time."

"That is just television," said George. "There is crime in Nairobi, and I am sure you have crime there in the states. But this is just a television show."

"I am glad to hear you say that," said Jeff. "Sometimes, in the U.S., we worry that the world knows us by our TV shows, and sometimes that's not a very pretty picture."

"I am sure that you know that Africa is not always the way you see it in movies."

"I do." He wasn't going to admit that a lot of Americans didn't.

"What do people know about Kenya back in the states?" asked George.

Axel perked up. "They know about your runners," he said. "And some of them know about the safari parks."

"What should we know about Kenya?" asked Jeff.

"There is more than one Kenya," said George. "Mombasa is not like Nairobi, and the north of Kenya is not like the west of Kenya."

"The borders of Africa were drawn in Europe, I'm afraid," said Jeff.

"I am proud of Kenya," said George. "I believe we are a nation, even though we are made up of many parts. We have a shared history, and a shared experience, as a British colony and now as a free nation. But too many people here in Nairobi think there is nothing but Nairobi and Mombasa. Pastor Joe knows that there is more, and he works with pastors from all over Kenya."

"I know he's bringing a lot of them in for the training next weekend," said Jeff.

"I am sorry we won't get to see more of your country," said Axel. "At least we will get to see more of it when we go to Masai Mara at the end of the trip."

No one was quite sure what time the others wanted to go to bed, and so after "CSI" everyone made noises about going to bed early, rather than keep the others up. As a result, Jeff would figure out later, everyone ended up going to bed about an hour earlier than they might have otherwise.

Once George, Elizabeth and Sally were upstairs, Axel and Jeff stretched out on their cots. Axel read through his water purification instructions for the umpteenth time, while Jeff wrote in his journal.

"I'm going to shower before bed," said Jeff. "Will that bother you?"

"Not at all," said Axel. "I'll shower in the morning."

"What time should we set the alarm for?"

"Six works for me."

"Works for me too."

## SIX
### Company's Coming

The team gathered for its meeting in the classroom which Schuyler would use later in the morning for her plastic crochet workshop.

"Did everyone sleep OK last night?" asked Teddy. "Are everyone's homes OK?"

"Let Schuyler do her devotion first, honey," said Dea.

"You're right. Schuyler?"

Schuyler's devotion was based on the story of Jesus sending out the disciples, two by two, in ministry. It was succinct and well-presented, Jeff thought.

"Do we have any prayer requests?" asked Schuyler before closing in prayer.

Dea confessed to being a little tired and wrung-out – probably nothing, she said, but she wanted prayers for stamina and prayers that she wouldn't come down with something serious.

"I've actually got my own prayer request," said Schuyler. "I finally got a hold of my husband last night.

"He told me he's moving out."

There was a collective gasp. Nothing like this had even been hinted at.

"We're hoping we can work through this, but he decided it would be better for us to spend some time apart, and he says it's less painful for him to move out now, while I'm away. I think it was sort of cowardly on his part, but there you go."

Teddy stood up.

"Let's have a special prayer for Schuyler," he said. "Gather around and let's lay hands on her." Schuyler stayed in her chair and the group clustered around her. Teddy prayed for strength, for reconciliation, and for Schuyler to be able to keep her focus on the task at hand.

"Is there anything practical we can do for you? Are you going to be OK with your workshop this morning?" asked Dea.

"I'll be fine. It's better to have something to focus on."

"I agree," said Teddy. "Let's move on for right now. Is everyone OK with their accomodations?"

"We're in better shape than I imagined us being when I signed up," said Lucy. "Joe and Helen have a very comfortable house, and we're in good shape."

"Do you have plenty of bottled water?"

"They have a big jug dispenser in the dining room, and they said it's safe – they have it delivered."

"No concerns with health, safety, anything like that?"

"None," said Lucy. "The only bad thing was that there's a mosque nearby, and the songs, or prayers, or whatever woke us up at 5 a.m."

"From what I understand," said Teddy, "Islam is growing here. I'm sorry about the noise. Did any of you bring earplugs?"

"I did," said Lucy.

"Me, too," said Schuyler.

"I didn't."

"Well, Kate, I think Dea or I may have an unused extra set in the first aid bucket that we can give you."

"Thank you."

"That's taken care of. Jeff, Axel?"

"We're good," said Jeff. "They sent our laundry out this morning to a neighborhood woman who does it by hand. And Sally's adorable. adorable. George brought us this morning, but I think Elizabeth and Sally are supposed to come later by matatu."

"OK," said Teddy. "We're in good shape, too.

"We're going to have worship at 9 a.m., and then the workshops will start after that. I told them to give you some extra setup time today between worship and the workshops, and so I think they're going to excuse us, just for today, from tea time."

"They have tea time?" asked Lucy.

"They do," said Dea. "This is a former British colony, and it's also a country that exports a lot of tea. They think of tea time as important, which means we have to treat it as important."

"Exactly," said Teddy. "All of our supplies are locked up in the church office. You can get them right after worship and move them to your classrooms.

"Oh – speaking of locked up. If you have to use the Mzungu Memorial Meditation Chamber, Dea has the key. Fellows, please use our designated stall even if you could, uh, use the other one standing up. They seem to be serious about this, and so let's just play along.

"Meanwhile, Dea and I will be working on preparations for the pastoral leadership training on Saturday. We'll be available if you need us for anything."

The meeting went through a few other routine items and then adjourned to the office. As the team was making its way, Jeff caught Schuyler's eye.

"You OK?"

"I'm gonna be."

"Let me know if you need me ... for anything. If

you need to vent, if you need me to take something over for you, if you just need to pummel me around a little bit. I am here."

"I appreciate it. What I need now is space."

"Understood. I love you, Schuyler."

Jeff was still shaken by the initial news. Rob and Schuyler had always seemed close, and content. Jeff loved listening to them banter, and tease each other, and finish each other's sentences. In a way, Jeff felt hurt that he'd poured out his frustrations to Schuyler during some of the times they'd spent together at church retreats or at pre-field training, and yet here was a gaping hole in her life that he knew nothing about.

*Well,* he told himself, *it's not like I would have wanted her telling me the details of her marriage. And it's not like I'm around her all the time. Why would I know about it?*

Then it occurred to Jeff – the fact that there was some distance between himself and Schuyler was part of the reason he felt comfortable opening up to her.

*Some of what I've told her, I'd never tell someone that I see every day.*

He caught a glimpse of Elizabeth and Sally in the courtyard and went out to meet them. So did Axel, and Sally ran gleefully toward Axel.

"Sorry about that, buddy. And here you are without any candy to bribe her with."

"My luck with women," said Jeff. "Typical."

The monochronic Americans drifted into the sanctuary as soon as they heard George, Elizabeth and the other worship leader begin to sing. *I'm late!* thought Jeff, even though he could clearly see most of the church members still milling about in the courtyard.

The team was deliberate about sitting throughout the sanctuary for morning worship, which seemed to disorient some of the church members, who weren't quite sure whether they were supposed to sit down next to the wazungu or not.

The service went well. Axel was called upon to give his testimony, and Dea preached, and both seemed well-received. Axel was a natural for speaking with a translator; he seemed to naturally speak in simple sentence structures and had a sense for when to stop talking and let the translator jump in.

At the end of the service, just before the closing prayer, Pastor Joe jumped in with logistics.

"We will ask everyone except our visitors to remain in the sanctuary for tea. Our visitors will have tea with us the rest of the week, but today they need this time to set up for their workshops, so we will take their tea to them in their classrooms. After the tea, we will begin our workshops."

Jeff went to the office to pick up his supplies and take them to his room. He saw Lucy struggling with her propane burner and grabbed it so that they could carry it between them.

"Have they shown you how to light this thing?" she asked.

"I have no clue," said Jeff. "I was going to ask one of my students to do it. I don't have enough hands-on stuff for everyone to do every day, so the more little tasks I can come up with, the better chance I have of involving everyone before the session is over."

"Good thinking." They set the burner down. "I still haven't found where they put my paraffin. I'm about to ask Joe."

Jeff was pleased to see his sodium hydroxide. The church had apparently bought a case of small plastic jars of the stuff from a chemical supply house. This was a manageable form – he didn't want to have to schlep around a 50-pound bag of a caustic chemical. He doubted they'd go through half of a jar during the week of workshops, but the church would have plenty left over to hopefully take up soap production on their own later.

*Hopefully. If I can teach them and not screw this up.*

One of the women of the church arrived with Jeff's tea. It was in a plastic cup not designed for hot beverages, and so the cup felt warm to the touch, but it didn't seem in danger of melting. The tea had been steeped in milk, or perhaps milk and water, and it was heavily sweetened. They brought a couple of cellophane-wrapped cookies along with the tea.

Jeff sipped at his sweet tea and looked at his

various supplies and materials. He seemed to have everything. He sat down.

Oscar came in.

"I will be your translator this week," he said.

"Thank you," said Jeff. "I will try to make things as easy on you as possible, but you should feel free to slow me down if I go too fast. I haven't worked with a translator before, so please be patient with me."

Oscar didn't seem to know how to respond to this; he shrugged, noncommittally.

In the courtyard, the students were lining up at a little table, where Helen was checking them off a hand-written list and telling them which classroom to go into.

Class members kept coming in to Jeff's room, and coming in, and coming in. He had expected about 10 or 12 class members; but soon, there were 25 people crammed into the little room, sitting on benches that were built for small children and standing around the edge of the room.

"Well ... um. Welcome, all of you."

After a couple of pleasantries, he moved on to what he had resolved weeks ago would be the very first part of his presentation.

"We will be working with a chemical called sodium hydroxide," he said. "I may call it lye by mistake; lye is the name for it in the United States. It is also known as caustic soda.

"This chemical can burn your skin or it can injure

your eyes. During our class, we will wear gloves and safety goggles whenever we handle the lye, and we will carefully wash any of our pots and pans that have been in contact with the lye.

"This spray bottle contains vinegar." The vinegar had been bought in Kenya, but no one in the class seemed to recognize the term; it apparently was not a very common ingredient. In fact, when Jeff looked at the label later in the week he would discover that it was *imitation* vinegar, whatever that might be.

Jeff was planning to leave behind safety goggles, but he hadn't brought 25 pair – and he wasn't at all sure that his students would spend money on latex gloves. But he was determined to at least operate safely during the class week, and try to convey some sense that lye was to be treated with respect.

He explained the basic process of combining fat and lye. He had someone light the burner and opened the plastic tub of beef tallow. It was a little bit darker than the lard he'd been using back in the states, and it didn't look anywhere near as well-refined. He knew that beef tallow could be substituted for lard in soap recipes, but he wondered if the soap would come out with a bad scent or texture.

"Soapmaking is a chemical formula," he said, "and so we must measure our ingredients by weight to make sure we have the right amount."

He had brought a very inexpensive plastic kitchen scale from a dollar store back in Tennessee. It had both English and metric measurements; he had, at least, thought in advance about the need to use metric measurements in Kenya.

"What if you do not have a scale?" asked one of the students.

"I will leave this scale here at the church, and so those of you who participate in the co-op that the church wants to establish will be able to use this scale. This is a very inexpensive type of scale."

Oscar went on long enough after this that Jeff suspected he was adding something to the remarks, perhaps talking about the church's plan to help set up a cooperative where the cottage industries could be practiced.

Jeff had a volunteer measure out the required amount of beef tallow and placed it in a stock pot over the fire to melt.

"This is a stainless steel pot," he said. "Some types of pots will not work for making soap because the lye – er, the sodium hydroxide -- will react to them. Aluminum pots will not work. Stainless steel *will* work, or a coated pot like this one" -- he pulled an enamel pot out of his suitcase -- "will work."

While the fat melted, he got a volunteer to measure the lye. Both he and the young man donned goggles and latex gloves. (Oscar was standing far enough to the side that Jeff didn't think he was at risk.) He sent another volunteer to get water in a measuring cup.

Jeff was pleased with the theatrical nature of the next moment. When the water came, he had both the volunteer who had measured the lye and the volunteer who had retrieved the water feel the side of the measuring cup. The water was cool.

Now, he had the lye volunteer stir the lye crystals into the water.

"It may stick to the bottom of the cup, so you will have to scrape it a bit as you stir."

Once the lye had been stirred in thoroughly, he had the volunteer feel the side of the cup again.

"It is hot!" he exclaimed.

"It is," Jeff agreed. "In fact, we usually want to let this water cool off a bit before we add it to the melted fat." Some hobbyist soapmakers in the U.S. were positively fanatic about temperature, believing that the melted fat and the lye water should be close to exactly the same temperature when combined. But others were far less concerned, and Jeff had made a decision not to obsess over temperature in this basic class.

Dea popped in with her camera to take a few shots. Jeff had pushed his goggles temporarily to the top of his head while waiting for the lye water to cool, but Dea had him put them back on and pose for a photo with his volunteer.

"Take one with my camera, too," said Jeff.

She did so, and then turned to the class members.

"Are you glad to be learning soapmaking?" she

asked.

They all nodded.

"Do you think this is something that you will be able to do after we have returned to the U.S.?"

Jeff thought to himself that this was a nearly-useless conversation. The Kenyans, out of courtesy, would no doubt have answered in the affirmative no matter what their thoughts.

*There's no real way to know for sure whether this will 'take' or not.*

After Dea had left, Jeff decided that the lye water had cooled down enough to mix with the melted fat. He called for a third volunteer, but no one seemed that anxious, so he let the young man who had stirred the lye into the water stir the lye water into the fat.

"We are mixing water and fat," said Jeff, "which normally separate. So we must keep stirring constantly to mix them together until the lye begins to combine with the fat. Once that happens, and the soap starts to form, it will bring the fat and the water together. But for the first half hour, we must stir constantly."

At home, Jeff would use a stick blender, and the mixture would come together in five minutes. Sirring by hand, he knew, it could take an hour, an hour and a half, or even longer, depending on temperature, the quality of the fat and how well it was stirred. But that was OK; it would fill time during the class, and he certainly didn't expect his students to have access to a stick blender.

"It will take some time for our mixture to turn into soap and begin to thicken. In the meantime, I have something else to show you."

He explained that while fragrances and colors were sometimes added during the soap-making process, it was not always possible to do so because the harsh alkalinity of the lye would change or simply neutralize the intended color or scent. So the other way to add ingredients was to grate down already-made soap and melt it over a double boiler.

He got a volunteer to put some water into the bottom of the enamel stock pot and another volunteer to begin grating some pieces of soap he had brought with him into a stainless steel bowl.

"Is this the type of soap we are making?" she asked.

"Yes, it is, except that this soap is made with pork fat instead of beef fat, because that is easier to buy in the United States."

"May I try a piece?" she asked.

"Uh ... sure. I have a sample piece for each of you." Jeff wasn't sure he would have enough samples to last all week if he had 25 people each day, but he decided to live dangerously rather than create a bad first impression.

He handed out the samples, and the woman who asked him for the soap, plus two others, darted out. Oscar looked at Jeff to see if he was annoyed or displeased by this, but Jeff just shrugged.

Jeff added a little bit of water to the grated soap and placed the metal bowl on top of the stock pot, making a double boiler.

"I can never get this to melt quite as perfectly smoothly as I would like. We will need to stir it so that it will heat evenly, but we don't need to stir it so much or so vigorously that it lathers up. We don't want it to lather until we use it."

He got a volunteer to gently stir the grated soap from time to time, and then asked how the stirring of the new batch of soap was going.

"I am continuing to stir," said his volunteer.

"What is your name?" asked Jeff. "I forgot to ask your name."

"I am Andrew Orina."

"It is good to meet you, Andrew. If you get tired and need someone else to stir for a while, just let us know. Why don't you sit down and put the pot on your lap, or on the floor in front of you?"

Andrew seemed to know English, but even so Oscar clarified the instructions in Swahili. Andrew placed the pot on the floor in front of him and continued to stir.

"We will know that the soap has formed, and is ready to pour into molds, when it gets so thick that when you pull the spoon through it, or dribble a little bit of the mixture on top of itself, it leaves a mark. That is called a 'trace,' and in soap making we say that when a soap is ready, it has 'traced.' Once a soap has traced, it is no longer in danger of separating into oil and water, and so you need to go ahead and pour it into a mold before it gets any thicker.

"But that won't happen for a while yet. Right now, while we're at a slow point, does anyone have any questions?"

A hand shot up. "Will we receive a certificate for this class?"

"A certificate? I don't know ... I'll have to check with Dea and Teddy on that."

The sample-soap women darted back in, beaming.

"We like the soap," said one of them. They held up their hands to indicate that they had been washed.

Unfortunately, at that point the discussion slowed to a crawl, and Jeff felt inadequate for not having brought more content. He started talking about the spiritual significance of soap, looked up passages in the Bible about being made clean, and talked about how, just as the fat reacts with the bitter sodium hydroxide to produce soap, Christ helped us to make the bitter things in our own lives into something new. But he felt like he was losing the class. He looked at Oscar but couldn't tell what his impression of the situation might be.

*I didn't bring enough content.*

It had been a while since the soap and the fat were mixed, so Jeff said it was no longer necessary to stir constantly; now, one could stir frequently, but set the mixture down and walk away from it to do something else from time to time. His volunteer seemed confused by this and continued to stir rather than risk catastrophe.

The grated soap, meanwhile, was not perfectly smooth, but Jeff had trouble getting it smooth even under the best of circumstances at home, so he decided to go ahead and try working with it. He had the students add a bit of grated crayon and a few drops of a lavender essential oil.

"Essential oils like these are very strong – and if you are trying to add fragrance while you are making the soap to begin with, essential oils are almost the only thing that will work even some of the time. But when you melt, or 'rebatch' the soap, you can add various types of fragrances – perfume, or perhaps you could even crush some flower or herb that you might have available in this area. Does anyone have an idea of something that you might use to add fragrance to the soap?"

Dead silence.

Jeff fumbled a long for a little while longer, and finally he saw that he was approaching the end of the class period.

The new soap had thickened somewhat but was still not at what Jeff would call trace. But he remembered what his teacher had told him; there were sometimes cases where the heat or the type of fat made tracing more difficult. He decided they would pour the soap anyway. He pulled out his plastic molds and had a volunteer pour the soap into each of them.

"Thank you very much for your attention today," Jeff said. "I hope this has been helpful."

As the students filed out, Oscar shook Jeff's hand.

"That was a very good teaching," said Oscar.

Jeff wasn't so sure.

◆

Jeff had asked about where to clean up his utensils, but they were snatched away by some of the church members before he could see about them. He told Oscar to make sure that they weren't being washed with food implements, and Oscar went to check on it.

Jeff collapsed on a bench in the courtyard. Lucy came over and sat next to him.

"How did it go?"

"I'm not satisfied."

"Schuyler didn't think you would be."

"What?"

"She told me last night, 'No matter how well Jeff's workshop goes, he'll think it was a failure.'"

"I'm not being neurotic. I just didn't see any light bulbs go on in the room today."

"Squint next time."

"Also, I don't think I brought enough for them to do."

"If you don't think they've picked up on what you've taught them so far, why are you in a hurry to move on to something different? Maybe repetition is exactly what you need. These aren't teenagers in a high school classroom. They want to be here. They want you to succeed."

Jeff scowled. "How was candle-making?"

"We had fun, I think. But we didn't make any candles."

"Why not?"

"Do you have any idea what the word 'paraffin' means in Kenya?"

"No ..."

"Kerosene. Kerosene here is called paraffin. What we call 'paraffin' in our country is short for 'paraffin wax,' and -- as it turns out -- I have no idea what they call it here. But I had asked them for paraffin, and so they brought me paraffin. A big jug of it."

"Oh, no."

"So we did not have the kind of wax we needed to melt to make candles."

"What did you do?"

"We talked. They asked me about the U.S., and I asked them about Kenya. Guy is going to try to find the wax, and so we'll get to it tomorrow."

Lunch had been prepared nearby, and it was set up in the courtyard: sukuma wiki and ugali, along with some flatbread. Joe blessed the food, and the Americans were urged to go through line first. Jeff was handed a full plate.

He took it back over to the bench where he and Lucy had been sitting and he started to eat.

It didn't taste bad ... it didn't taste that different from what had been served the first night at St. Martin's. Taste was not the problem. Jeff was not exactly sure what the problem was.

But there was a problem. Maybe it was the mental picture of big kettles of food in the dusty courtyard. Maybe it was the dirty smoky scent that Jeff smelled in the courtyard and which seemed to permeate the area. Jeff had a violent gag reflex to the sukuma wiki, the same kind he'd had when he was a child and took a mouthful of some food he hated, like beets or cauliflower. With great difficulty, he forced the first bite down.

He took a bite of bland ugali and washed it down with bottled water. He took another bite of ugali, then a bite of flatbread. Then he took a bite of sukuma wiki.

He thought he was going to choke, or start into a coughing fit. He couldn't swallow it. He walked around beside one of the buildings, out of sight, and spit it into the dirt.

He had worried about the food in advance ... was this psychosomatic? Self-fulfilling? Surely, it was all in his head. As he walked back into the courtyard, he saw everyone else, American and Kenyan alike, enjoying the food without any problem. But his stomach was turning cartwheels.

He walked up to Axel.

"How are you liking the food?" Jeff asked.

"Much better than what we had that first night," Axel said.

Jeff tried to stomach a few more bites of ugali and flatbread, but he couldn't make himself eat any more sukuma wiki.

Trying to act nonchalant, he walked up to Dea.

"Jeff! Doris was telling me how much she enjoyed the soapmaking workshop.

"Good. Dea ... I'm having trouble with the food, and I don't know why."

"We can talk about it later."

"Right. But what do I do with my plate? I know you told us not to waste anything.

"Give it to me. I'll make sure they give it to one of the orphans or someone who's still hungry."

Jeff felt both relieved and guilty.

He wandered around and saw Schuyler, who had been eating with several of the women, standing up.

"Do you know where we take our empty plates?" Schuyler asked.

"No, I don't," said Jeff.

"Where did you take yours?"

"Somebody took mine." He scratched his scalp. "So ... how was your morning?"

"Great. The women were just delighted at the idea of crocheting with plastic bags. Some of them crochet or do something similar already and they're great at it. What they're doing already looks a lot better than the samples I brought with me. And it's just the first day!"

"Where's Kate?"

"A lot of people are eating in the sanctuary, and Kate is in there sitting with some of the kids."

Helen came up to Joe and Schuyler.

"If you want to come into the office, we have something for you," she said.

It turns out there was a small refrigerator in the office – the type that college students keep in their dorm rooms in the U.S. Inside were soft drinks, and a bottle opener was on top.

Lucy was already in the office, sipping on a Coke, and Jeff and Schuyler eagerly joined her.

"What's up next?" Lucy asked.

"I think we're going to visit a few homes in the slums."

◆

"We will break up into teams," said Pastor Joe. "Two visitors will go with two of our members, except that Teddy will go with me and two others."

Jeff and Kate were put onto a team with Andrew Orina, who had stirred the soap that morning, and a woman from the church named Carol.

The teams headed down the street from the church, through some of the dusty little storefronts leading towards the Kibera slums. They crossed a railroad track, and the residential area started, literally, on the other side of the tracks.

The houses were built of what appeared to be mud, and had tin roofs. They were quite close together, and the dirt between them was deeply rutted, with water standing or running in some of the ruts.

At least, Jeff hoped it was water. His nose told him otherwise.

Children were running about in the narrow streets. One was pulling a toy vehicle which had been carefully crafted out of a paper carton – like a child's juice box, only larger; Jeff thought he'd seen chicken stock in boxes like that back home. It had little cardboard wheels and was pulled by a a string.

Another boy was rolling a hoop along the street with a stick. Jeff had seen drawings of boys back in the days of Tom Sawyer and Huck Finn rolling a hoop, pushing it along by tapping it with a stick, trying to keep it upright and in motion. This was exactly the same kind of hoop.

Andrew led his team to its first house. The rough door was open, and Andrew called in. He got a friendly response.

"Do these people know we're coming?" Kate whispered to Jeff.

"I have no idea."

Andrew, Jeff, Kate and Carol crammed into the home's little living room, which was separated by a sheet from the rest of the house. There were plastic stacking chairs – the type you might use in your backyard in the U.S.

A weary young woman inside the dim house gestured for everyone to sit down.

"Welcome," she said. An extremely elderly-looking woman came out from the back room and appeared delighted with her visitors. Andrew spoke to her briefly in Swahili, then switched to English:

"Our visitors from America here are speaking at the church each day. This is Jeff and this is Kate."

"Pleased to meet you," said Jeff, and Kate made pleasantries as well.

"Perhaps," said Andrew, "the visitors from America would like to pray for you."

"Yes!" said Jeff, happy for the hint. "What would you like us to pray for?" The younger woman translated this into Swahili for the older woman, who responded in plaintive tones, and in Swahili. Andrew translated.

"She wants you to pray for her daughter, here, who has AIDS."

Jeff and Kate looked at each other. The woman with AIDS was the young woman who'd first welcomed them to the house. Kate stood and knelt down in front of the young woman, placing a hand on her knee. Jeff, following Kate's lead, walked over and stood behind the woman, with his hands on her shoulders.

"What is your name?" Kate asked.

"Naomi." She appeared uncomfortable and her eyes had started to tear up a little bit as the group turned its attention to her.

Kate began praying for Naomi, and then Jeff followed. It was a fervent prayer, more fervent in some ways than Jeff was used to praying. It was a prayer for healing, but if not for healing, for relief, and knowledge of God's presence. Andrew did not bother to translate, and Jeff hoped that Naomi was able to follow what was being said even if her mother could not.

Jeff had, even as he was praying for the woman, thoughts of which he was not proud – thoughts of blame, worries about whether he, or she, had any open sores, annoyance that no one had told them about this in advance.

"... in Jesus' name. Amen."

Naomi hugged Kate, and Jeff. Her grasp was weak, but Jeff truly felt embraced.

Kate wanted to talk more to Naomi about the disease. She had been to see a doctor, who had told her that she had AIDS, but she could not get into a hospital until the later stages of the disease. But Andrew said it was time to move to the next home.

"I think she actually has HIV," Kate said, so only Jeff could hear, as they walked to the next house. "It hasn't gone into AIDS yet. She may not be having any symptoms now, but if she's been diagnosed, she should be getting some sort of treatment, especially if she feels bad."

"Did you read up on this?" Jeff asked.

"I did, actually. I was on the Internet trying to figure out what shots I needed and I ended up looking up the AIDS figures for Africa. There's no risk from casual contact."

"I know. I know. But sometimes it's hard to give up the old wives' tales."

"If you were worried," said Kate, "you sure didn't show it."

Andrew, who had been leading the way and talking to Carol about something, dropped back to speak to Jeff.

"You pray powerfully," he said.

*You must be easily impressed,* thought Jeff.

On the way to the next home, they passed a home where people were working on stringing together little beaded items, not unlike some of the souvenirs Jeff had seen at the Maasai market, including some of the ones he thought might have been made in China.

On the other hand, these people didn't seem to be Maasai. But maybe "Maasai market" was just a name.

The next home had a mother, a father, and five children. None of them had come to the church that morning, so Kate made a point of inviting them to attend the workshops and talking to them about all of the fun things she would lead the children in doing the next day.

"Do all of these children live here?" Jeff asked.

"Yes," said Andrew. "The whole family."

It was smaller than a dorm room, a tiny place for just one person in the U.S.

"Are these homes made from mud?" Jeff asked Andrew, as they stepped outside.

"Mud and cow dung. The cow dung makes it strong so that it does not wash away during the rainy season."

"I don't see any cows."

Before Jeff could solve the mystery of where the cow dung came from, Andrew hailed a friend he met in the street.

While Andrew, Carol and his friend talked, Jeff looked around at the houses.

"How do people live like this?" he asked Kate. "I mean, how do people live like this?" As he breathed in the smell of sewage, he felt sick to his stomach.

"Think about how they were dressed in church yesterday," said Kate. "Some of them looked really nice. How do they keep their clothes clean?"

Andrew finished his conversation and directed them on to the next house.

As the group waled into the third house, there were a woman and two children waiting. Andrew went over and stood next to the woman.

"Welcome to my home," he said, beaming. "This is my wife, Maria, and my children, Charity and Thomas."

"It is an honor to be here," said Jeff.

"Charity and Thomas were with me earlier," said Kate.

They sat in more plastic stacking chairs and Maria brought out bottled water for Jeff, Kate and Carol. Jeff wondered how much it cost and how much it represented compared to a day's wages for Andrew.

"Jeff is teaching me how to make soap," said Andrew to Maria, "and Kate is working with the children."

"I sent the children to church this morning," said Maria. "I wanted to go myself, but I had to take care of some things here. I will be at church tomorrow."

Jeff looked at the sheet which divided the little home in two and wondered what the "bedroom" must be like on the other side of it. There could barely be room for everyone to lay down at the same time.

"Andrew is a much better student than I am a teacher," said Jeff.

"No," he said, "you are a wonderful teacher. I want to learn and make many bars of soap to sell in the market."

Jeff's nose was running, and he picked up his backpack and rooted around for the roll of toilet paper Axel had given him. He dabbed at his nose as politely as he could, then took a big swig of bottled water.

He and Kate looked at each other.

"Thomas, Charity," said Kate. "Do you remember

the song we sang today?"

◆

"He was just so proud to have us as his guests," said Jeff. "I had just been talking to Kate about how anyone could live like that, and he's showing off his home and he's so proud to have us there. I started to tear up, but I don't think he noticed."

"It's early in the week, Jeff," said Teddy, "maybe too early for a discussion of lessons learned. But for me, that's been a constant challenge. The poverty in which these people live is a terrible, terrible thing, with real consequences in terms of education, and comfort, and medical care. You said the AIDS patient you talked to can't get into the hospital until the later stages of the disease. Maybe she won't get in then. She can't afford it, and maybe there won't be enough charity beds available.

"If poverty weren't real, if it didn't have consequences, we wouldn't be here trying to help.

"But the joy that some of these people have, in the middle of all this poverty, is a very humbling thing. It challenges us. We want to say, 'Well, that's all they've ever known, so of course they're satisfied with it.' But that's wrong. Living here on the edge of a city like this, they see how the people of Nairobi live. They hear things about how people live in countries like ours. They know there is something better out there, and they want something better. And yet, they are able to have joy in their situation.

"As we told you at training, you are here not only to teach but to learn. I think you had a powerful lesson today."

"I hope I learned it."

"Now, I *am* concerned that you were taken to the home of an AIDS patient without warning. I will talk to Joe about that. I'm responsible for your safety and security, and we should have known about something like that in advance."

"I think it worked out OK. We weren't at any risk."

"I still feel responsible."

"Responsible for what? *There was no risk.* Plus, I think God wanted us to be there."

Teddy looked at Jeff for a moment and grinned.

"Jeff, I've started to think of myself as some sort of expert on foreign missions. But sometimes it occurs to me that I don't know anything."

◆

Jeff walked from the office out into the courtyard. Lucy and Kate were sitting on a bench, talking. Kate looked up and saw Jeff.

"Hey," said Kate. "I was just telling Lucy about Andrew's house. I could tell it was getting to you."

"I just had the sniffles."

"I think we both had the sniffles."

"So, Lucy, how was your visitation?"

"Okay, I guess," said Lucy. "I'm not good at praying for people."

"That's what *I* keep trying to tell people. I'm no good at praying for people either."

## SEVEN
<u>Would You Lye To Me, Baby?</u>

Axel was somewhat subdued as he and Jeff rode with Sally in the back seat of George and Elizabeth's car.

"Are you okay?" Jeff asked.

Axel put up his hand in a "stop" gesture and silently mouthed the word, "later."

They stopped at a convenience store to fill up the car.

"I am so sorry," said George. "I should have gotten gas today while you were at the church."

Actually, Jeff was thrilled to be able to wander through the convenience store. He bought an

unfamiliar African soft drink – Stoney Tangawizi --
and some hard candy for later. The Stoney Tangawizi
was a citrusy drink but with a slight spicy, almost
cinnamon, aftertaste. It was quite good, actually.

When they got home, Elizabeth said that dinner
would be ready in 45 minutes and Jeff and Axel went
into their room.

"What's up?" asked Jeff.

"You know, buddy, when I first met the orphans
at the church I felt sorry for them, having to live in
those little rooms. Then I saw where they'd be living
if it weren't at the church. I guess it just got to me. I'll
be OK."

"I know. It got to me, too. We saw a woman with
AIDS in one of our houses today."

"I want to spend the night there before we leave."

"In the slums?"

"Yeah. I'm going to ask Teddy tomorrow."

"I don't think they'll let you do it, Axel."

"I'm going to ask anyway."

"Who were you with today?"

"I was with Lucy," said Axel, "and George was
our team leader."

"Lucy didn't have much to say afterward."

"Well, one of the women we went to see was
pregnant, and they asked Lucy to pray for her, and I
think it may have bothered her a little bit."

"I hate to hear that. How did the water go
today?"

"Pretty good. We explained to them how the system works, and they're supposed to be getting the gravel and the sand for the filtration barrels. We started building a stand for the supply tank – it's got to be above the other tanks, so that the water can flow downhill. They found some lumber, and of course all they had were hand tools, but it came together OK. I'm hoping we can get all of the pipes and plumbing hooked together tomorrow."

"Sounds like you're making progress."

"I hope so. How was soapmaking?"

"It went smoothly enough, but I don't know if I'm really connecting with them. I don't know if I can see them doing this after I leave."

"It was just the first day. Things will turn around, I bet you."

"I hope you're right," said Jeff. "How do you think Schuyler is doing?"

"I think she's OK. She kept busy today, and that was a good thing. It's right now, in the evenings, that she'll be tempted to dwell on it, but hopefully Kate and Lucy can keep her from sinking too far."

"She always seems like a positive person, and she's always been so good at encouraging me – but after hearing this, I wonder how well I really know her at all."

"You know her. She didn't talk about it because she *is* such a positive person. It's not that it's a huge secret or anything; she just doesn't unload on people."

"I unload on everybody."

"Well, buddy, that's because you're by yourself. You got nobody to unload on, so you unload on everybody."

"You have me pegged there."

"So ... when are you going to say something to Lucy?"

"About what?"

"Don't give me that. I've seen those puppy-dog eyes the whole trip. You, my friend, are interested."

"I probably am. But this isn't the time or the place. Maybe it's just because we're so far from home, and I do feel kind of alone, and she's the only woman on the trip who's unattached and in my age range."

"I'm not saying you should sweep her off her feet and take her to dinner. Like you say, we're here to work. But that doesn't mean you can't get to know her a little better in the process."

"I've tried. I tried at pre-field. And she's always been really nice to me, but whenever I try to talk about her, or anything serious, she clams up and remembers somewhere she needs to be. She's not interested, at least not in me."

"You know what your problem is, Jeff? You think too much."

There was nothing Jeff could say to that.

◆

Dinner was small sausages – Jeff assumed they must have been beef, given what he'd heard about disdain for pork in Kenya – and rice, with some orange wedges as well.

Jeff turned to George during the meal. "How do you think today went?"

"I think everyone was very pleased. I have heard many good comments about the workshops. And I am excited that the water system is progressing."

"Have you heard anything that we need to do differently tomorrow? Anything that we might not understand, coming from a different country?"

"No."

Jeff expected that answer.

"I am asking you seriously, honestly. It will help us to know how we can improve what we are doing."

"I will think about that."

"Please do."

"George," Axel said, "you have a phone here, right?"

"Yes."

"I have a card to call home to the U.S. It shouldn't cost you anything more than a local call – the long distance will be billed to me back home. Would you mind if I called my wife tonight?"

"No, not at all."

"I'll wait until just before bedtime – I think that should be a good time to reach her at work."

"That will be fine."

"I appreciate it. I miss her, and I know she's worried about me – about all of us."

"Worried?"

"Oh, just us being so far from home, in a strange place."

"I see." He turned to Jeff. "So ... Axel has mentioned his wife. But, Jeff, you are not married?"

"No."

"Have you been married?"

"No. I am not ... I am not very good with women. The ones I'm attracted to aren't attracted to me."

"My grandfather used to tell me it was selfish for a man to live alone," said George.

"Your grandfather was probably right."

"But you don't seem selfish to me. You have come all this way to help people."

"I'm trying not to be so selfish," said Jeff.

"He doesn't quite know what he's talking about," said Axel. "But he's pretty much harmless."

"I think he does know what he is talking about," said George. "Andrew and Oscar said the soap workshop was very informative."

"Well, our boy here is a little unsure of himself. He doesn't think he taught them enough."

"My favorite teacher once said to me that it is better to learn a simple thing well than to forget five complicated things. You are teaching a simple thing, and teaching it well. That is something to be proud of, and that is what the people in Kibera need."

◆

The next morning, Jeff used up the last of the

clothing in his suitcase. The laundry he'd sent off to be hand-washed Monday morning had not come back yet, and Jeff had resolved that he wasn't going to ask about it. But he hoped it would get back that day so that he would have clean clothes.

It was Lucy's turn to lead the team meeting on Tuesday morning. She called on Axel for the devotional. Axel's devotional came straight out of a popular Christian book which everyone in the room had either already read or had heard their preachers quote from the pulpit. But it was hard to fault Axel's enthusiasm, and at least he had picked a good, and relevant, story.

He also told the group that Denise said it was sunny and blisteringly hot in Tennessee, as opposed to the mild weather at high altitude in Nairobi, with highs in the mid-70s every day of the trip.

Lucy then resumed the meeting.

"Well, I am pleased to announce that there is now wax in my classroom."

"We're glad to hear it," said Schuyler.

"Now," said Lucy, "How did things go yesterday?"

"It was a good first day," said Schuyler. "Typical ups and downs, but we all got through it OK."

"How was the visitation in the slums yesterday afternoon?"

"Moving," said Dea.

"Heart-breaking, and yet ... joyful," said Jeff.

Teddy mentioned the woman with AIDS and passed out a fact sheet on AIDS in Africa which he'd managed to download from the Internet.

"We mentioned AIDS during the pre-field training, but looking back I don't think we did enough with it. So here's some background information for you about the severity of the problem, and on the back some information on what is safe and not safe for you as a visitor. Most of it's common sense, and the behaviors that put you at risk aren't anything any of you would be doing on this trip anyway. But it's important information to have, and to familiarize yourself with.

"We should have touched base on this issue with Joe and Helen, and we didn't, and we should have dealt with it more during training, and we didn't, and we were caught by surprise."

"Honestly," said Kate, "it wasn't a problem."

Axel spoke up. "What are the chances of getting to spend a night in the slums? I mean, Jeff and I are sitting in the living room at night watching American shows on TV. I'd like to be able to spend a night with the people down in the slums."

"I'm afraid that's out of the question," said Teddy, "and let me tell you why. Not only would it be an incredible security risk for you while you were there overnight, but if you made it through the night OK, the following night, after you had gone, whoever you were staying with in the slums would be robbed.

People would know that they had had American visitors and some might assume that you had left them money or valuables."

"Speaking of which," added Dea, "let me go back to something we said during pre-field. You have all bought small, symbolic gifts to give to your host families at the end of the week. Let me re-state that you should not, *not*, give any money to individuals during this trip, no matter what the situation. It would cause jealousy and division, and we are not going to do it.

"If there is any particular situation that you feel moved to do something about, come see us and we can funnel the money through the church. If you want to give money once you get back to the states, we can funnel that money through the church as well. Joe has a checking account in the U.S. that he uses when he comes to America to raise support. We can deposit money into it in the U.S. and he can write a check or use an ATM here in Nairobi.

"But giving money, even what you would consider a small amount of money, to individuals is going to cause problems."

"A friend of mine took a mission trip here last year," said Lucy, "and after he got back he got e-mails from one or two people asking him from money. He had no idea how they even e-mailed him."

"There are Internet cafés here," said Dea, "and it's easy to set up a free webmail account. Yes, you may get a message like that after you get home, or someone may ask you for money while you're here. And you obviously care about these people and their situation, or you wouldn't be here. But handing out dollars, or shillings, is going to cause more harm than you realize."

The group took this in.

"Okay," said Lucy. "Other questions?"

Jeff raised his hand. "One of my students asked about a certificate yesterday."

"So did one of mine," said Lucy. "Any idea what they're talking about?"

"Apparently," said Teddy, "there are some regulations governing the sale of products here in Kenya. You have to be able to show that you've had the proper training. Unfortunately, especially in your soap-making class, Jeff, we are not going to be giving enough individual hands-on experience, and we're not going to be testing people at the end of the week. So we're not in a position to give out any certificates. Tell your people that's something the church is going to have to work out after we leave."

"OK."

"All right," said Lucy. "Teddy, Dea, do you have anything else?"

"Yes," said Dea, "a couple of things. This afternoon, after lunch, we're going to be going into the slums to do some street ministry. The skit we rehearsed last weekend of the Prodigal Son, let's do that, and then Teddy is going to give a very short message, and one of the people from the church may give a short message.

"Also – let's be careful about lunch. It's good that the church has taken care of us with the Cokes, and I had one yesterday just like everyone else, but we don't need to camp out for too long in the office. We don't need to turn that space into a VIP tent. Let's mingle as much as we can, and if you want to go in the office and get a Coke, do that, but let's not all of us spend too long in there at the same time.

"That's all I've got."

"Okay," said Lucy. "Would someone like to pray for our day?"

◆

After the meeting, Jeff went to the office – where all of the workshop items had been stored – to retrieve his soapmaking paraphernalia. He was pleased to see that the soap he had poured yesterday had hardened up nicely despite having been poured short of trace. It wasn't quite yet hard enough to un-mold, but Jeff had brought enough extra molds for a second day.

Morning worship was relatively uneventful. The team drifted in a little bit later, but still early, and church members felt a little more comfortable sitting with the American team.

Teddy told the story of his alcoholism, and it obviously seemed to resonate with some in the crowd.

After the worship, the team – who had less setting up to do – took their tea with the group.

"Perhaps at the end of your trip – when you go on what you call a safari – as you see some of the countryside, you will pass some of the tea plantations and see where our Kenyan tea is grown," Joe told Jeff and Schuyler as they sat and took their tea among a group of Kenyans.

Then, it was time to go to workshops, and Jeff found Andrew already in the classroom waiting for him.

Andrew was holding two long, scored bars of soap like the ones Jeff had seen in the market a few days earlier.

"I want to make bars like these," said Andrew. "This is how we buy soap here in Kenya. Will you show us how to make bars like these?"

Jeff took one of the bars and looked at it.

"Let's wait until the rest of the group gets here."

When the class was gathered and ready to start, Jeff got them started on the same process as the day before. Jeff was relieved to see that it was mostly the same students as the day before, but even so he planned for the basic outline of the class to be the same. Repetition was good, Dea had said, especially when cultural or language differences might keep something from being fully communicated the first time around.

Once the fat was melting and the lye water was cooling, Jeff held up the bar Andrew had brought.

"Andrew has asked me if we can make a bar of soap shaped like this. Our purpose here is to help you make a product that you can sell, but you know far better than I what will sell here and what will not. If this is how people buy soap here, then perhaps we should make soap that looks like this. Or perhaps making something different, like the bars we made yesterday – he picked up one of the previous day's bars, still in the mold – will catch people's attention. What do you think?"

Once Oscar had translated all of this, the class members were unanimous in agreeing with Andrew's idea.

"Then that's what we'll do. Wait here a minute. Andrew – come with me."

They went to find Axel at the water purification workshop. Axel and Teddy were watching as sand was being shoveled into a plastic barrel.

"Axel."

"What's up, buddy?"

"If you have a free moment, at some time, I have a favor to ask."

"Shoot."

"I need a simple wooden frame that will fit snugly around this bar of soap."

"That's a long bar of soap."

"That's how they sell it here, and that's how my

class wants to make it."

"So this is a mold?"

"That's the idea. I think all we need is an open frame – the woman who taught me soapmaking had a frame sort of like this that she used for some of her bars. You set the frame flat down on the table and pour soap into it, and the soap is thick enough that it stays within the frame and doesn't ooze out the bottom – at least, not enough to matter. Then, when the soap hardens, you just take your thumbs and push it out of the frame."

"We can fix you up. When do you need it?"

"If you get it done by the end of our period, we'll pour it today. If not, we'll use our regular molds and try this one tomorrow. I know your first priority is the water."

"I think we have enough extra manpower that we can get this done for you."

Teddy grinned. "Synergy in action – I love it!"

Just then, there was a commotion coming from the classroom. Jeff sprinted back to find one of the students, a teenage boy, with his hands over his eyes. Oscar was standing next to him, his arms around him.

Jeff's blood ran cold.

"TEDDY! DEA!" he yelled. "What happened?"

Everything he had read and everyone he had spoken to before the trip had stressed the importance of wearing safety goggles and the danger of being blinded by lye. You were always supposed to add lye to water, rather than the other way around, because of the danger that the lye might bubble up and erupt out of the mixing vessel.

But the lye and water had already been mixed, correctly, before Jeff left the class.

Fortunately, what had happened was not exactly what Jeff had feared. There had apparently been a little bit of water in the stockpot used to melt the beef tallow, and the tallow had gotten a little too hot in Jeff's absence, causing it to spatter. The teenager, Tony, had been looking into the pot and had been caught on the eyelids, the eyebrows and the bridge of his nose by a spatter of grease. His skin was burned but apparently not his eyes.

Dea came and took Tony to the office, where she was keeping the team's first aid kit.

Jeff tried to resume the workshop, but his knees felt as if they were going to give out beneath him. He sat down and took the chance to repeat his safety speech from the previous day.

When he went to resume the soap-making process, he noted that the tallow had been allowed to get very hot, and it wasn't well-refined, so it had broken down a little and turned a deeper gold color than expected. Jeff wondered if this would affect its SAP value, the ratio at which it combined with lye to form soap, but he had no idea.

He had little choice at that point but to forge on ahead. After determining that the oil had cooled off somewhat, he let the students stir the lye water into it.

While the new soap from the previous day wasn't yet ready to be unmolded, the rebatched soap was. Its texture was not perfect – it had a curd-like appearance and texture, like cottage cheese made into a bar. And it was still a little soft – because of the water which had been added to help melt the soap, which now needed to air dry. He explained all this to the students but passed the bars around so that they could feel them.

They made some more rebatched soap and put it into the same molds.

Someone asked how soon it would take for the newly-made soap to be unmolded.

"We can probably unmold it tomorrow," said Jeff. "But you won't be able to use it for a month."

Every brow in the room furrowed.

"I know that's frustrating. But because this is cold process soap, there is a a possibility that there is still some unreacted lye hiding in there. By giving the soap a month to cure, you give that lye a chance to react with the remaining fat. Even though the soap will seem hard and ready to use, it's important to wait, or else you may find that the soap is too alkaline and that it irritates your skin when you use it.

"That's even more important if you are trying to sell the soap, because you would not want your customers to have a problem with it and then blame you."

"You must wait a month?" asked Oscar.

"Yes."

"No less?"

"No less. Actually, some of the sources I read want you to wait six weeks, but I think a month will be sufficient."

An older man in the back of the room said something in Swahili.

"It is like planting seed," translating Oscar, "and waiting for a crop."

"Exactly!" said Jeff. But he could tell the class was still disappointed at this unwelcome news.

"You will be able to use the rebatched soap as soon as it dries, because it was already cured before you melted it down."

Just as the class was winding down, a runner from the water workshop arrived with not one but two frames, as well as the original bar of soap. The molds were laid flat on the teacher's desk, and Jeff watched with pride as the class members poured soap into each of them.

Jeff turned to Oscar.

"We will need to leave those there. We can't pick them up and move them into the office with the rest of the supplies, or the soap will just run out the bottom. We need to leave them there and make sure no one touches them for the next few hours, or preferably not until tomorrow."

"I will see to it."

"And I can wash the pots and pans. It's not necessary for the church to do it."

"We will take care of the washing. You take care of the teaching."

The children's activities had broken up – the kids were milling about in the courtyard – and Jeff was gathering up his supplies to put into the office when Kate stuck her head into the room.

"Jeff ...."

"Yes?"

"Did I hear you say that a little lye would help keep the outhouse from smelling so bad?"

Jeff made up some lye water and poured half of it into each stall.

"Thank you, thank you, thank you," said Kate.

"No problem."

◆

Jeff talked the woman in the serving line into giving him smaller portions of food for lunch. Today, there was rice, and cabbage, and some small and gristly pieces of meat. Jeff didn't have nearly as much trouble with it. However, as a precaution he was sitting by himself in a chair over in the corner of the courtyard.

Schuyler dragged a chair over and sat next to him.

"I heard you had some excitement today in soap-making."

"Someone got hit in the face with hot grease. I

was afraid it was lye, which could have blinded them. And I mean blinded."

"Well, it all worked out OK. Dea said the boy's burns aren't that bad, and she's put some ointment on them."

"I know – but I guess it scared me. It made me think of what could have happened. And it would have been my fault."

"How, exactly, would it have been your fault?"

"It's like everybody else who comes to Africa trying to help. We have high ideals, but things fall apart."

"I see. Your soapmaking workshop is a symbol of the colonialization of Africa."

"That's not what I meant."

"Jeez, Jeff, it's getting a little old. You've come here trying to help. You've prepared yourself as best you can, you're doing the best job you can, and you were willing to make the trip. No one expects you to be Mother Teresa. You're here trying to do good. And you are doing good. And you're learning things about this place that you can take back to our place, and when somebody back home talks about poverty, or economics, or trade, you can tell them you've been to the Kibera slums and they don't know what the h— heck they're talking about."

"Okay."

"I know that 'Okay.' It means you're not really listening. You're discounting me even as I sit here talking to you.

"People love you, Jeff. What's more than that, people respect you. Why is it so hard for you to accept that?"

"I'll try."

"Don't just try."

"How are you doing? How was crochet today?"

"It's going very well. They're going faster, and the pattern is looking better. And I'm doing fine. As much as I hate to admit it, I think Rob may have been right about it being easier this way. He knows me pretty well."

◆

"Teddy," asked Axel, "I have some tracts that some friends of mine gave me to bring on the trip. Is it OK if I give them out when we get to where we're doing the street ministry?"

"I wish you'd have talked to me about this sooner, Axel. What kind of tracts?"

Axel, Jeff and Teddy walked together as a group of 20 – all of the Americans plus 13 Kenyans -- headed from the church towards the intersection that the church had picked out for the street preaching.

There were a variety of designs in the stack Axel pulled from his pocket, including the old-reliable fake currency: tracts that looked like a folded-up $20 or $100 bill, left on the floor in public places, in the hopes that passers-by would pick them up – and then, Jeff suspected, immediately throw them back down again. Jeff was not a fan of tracts, which he thought were simplistic and tended to leave people with a bad impression of Christianity. But it was hard for him to be too critical of them because he felt guilty that he'd never been active in sharing his faith with others.

*At least someone like Axel is trying to make a difference*, Jeff thought.

"Axel," said Teddy, "why don't you hold on to these? I want to make sure there's nothing in them that's not going to translate well. Sometimes, a catchy slogan or gimmick that works back in the States might not mean anything – or might mean something bad – in another culture. We'll look at them later and maybe find a way for you to use some of them later in the trip."

Axel was disappointed but stuffed the tracts back into his pocket.

The intersection where the church members wanted to stop and set up was an odd one – a convergence of three different streets, but on one of the corners there was a tremendous pile of garbage, with a footprint about 10 feet square.

It had been decided that, rather than try to translate dialogue as it was being spoken, Dea and a translator would read the Prodigal Son story aloud while the cast – Teddy as the father, Jeff as the older brother and Axel as the prodigal – acted it out, wordlessly.

"If we'd had a little more time," said Teddy, "I

would loved to have gotten some of the church members involved in the skit."

But as it was, it went smoothly enough. Axel camped up the role of the prodigal son, which seemed to be well received by those paying attention.

Many didn't pay attention. Some passers-by just ignored the strange group of Americans play-acting in the street. Had they seen this type of thing before? Jeff wondered. Or did they just not know what to make of it? Maybe they were offended by proselytizing. Maybe they just didn't want to hang around the stench of the garbage pile.

After the skit, Dea began talking about the message of the story. A man from the nearby spectators began yelling at her, in Swahili, and several of the church members went over and started to converse with him. They seemed to surround him and force him out of the way. Jeff had no idea what was going on and hoped it was nothing that that he'd be ashamed of.

Dea reclaimed the group's focus and continued her explanation of the story. Joe then spoke briefly about the church (in Swahili – but one of the church members translated it in hushed tones for the Americans standing nearby). He introduced Guy, who preached a brief message and ended with an altar call, but also a call for people to come to services at the church the next day.

There really didn't seem to be that much

response, and Axel asked Joe about this as they were walking back to the church.

"We are planting seeds, Axel. God will bring the harvest." Axel wasn't completely satisfied with this answer (and Jeff could tell Axel thought that his tracts would have made good fertilizer for the crop).

Lucy and Kate were engaged in some sort of animated conversation as they walked together. Teddy, Dea and Schuyler were each conversing with church members. Jeff walked silently, hanging behind a little bit. He noticed one of the dingy little shops – from the street, it looked like the size of a closet – sold cell phones, accessories and scratch-off pre-paid calling cards. It looked strange to see here in the middle of the slums, but Jeff had to remind himself that these weren't the same flashy cell phones for which people were signing up back home.

When the group got back to the church, Jeff got someone to let him into his classroom room so that he could sneak a peek at the long bars of soap. It was doing just fine – it had solidified enough that there was no danger of it oozing out.

"Is that your soap?" asked Lucy, who had walked in behind him. It startled him, and he jerked.

"I'm sorry," Lucy said.

"It's OK. Yes, this is the soap. We made these long bars because they're what people are used to buying around here." One of the sample bars was still sitting nearby on the table. "You see, you can break off individual bars at these score marks.

"The score marks! That's what I need to do, while the soap is soft." He fumbled in his pocket for a blue stick pen – he kept one with him at all times in case he needed to journal – and popped off the cap. The pocket clip extended from the end of the cap like a ponytail, and it was triangle-shaped. Jeff used it to draw neat little grooves across the soap every few inches.

"There."

"Looks good. You're doing a good job here."

*How does she know? She's not seen me teach. She's busy with her own workshop. I have soap, but I could make soap by myself. She doesn't know whether I'm a good teacher or not.*

"Thanks. But I was upset today; one of my students got hurt, and I was really scared about it at first."

"But it came out OK."

"It did. How are you doing?"

"The candle-making workshop is going very well."

"That's not exactly what I asked. How are you doing?"

Lucy stopped and thought about this for a second.

"I'm doing OK. I just feel so privileged to be here. And so humbled. And so ... well, it's hard to look at something like the Kibera slums and not question yourself a little bit. Especially if your job is talking people into trading their big home for a bigger one."

"I know." There were two chairs over against one wall, and Jeff sat in one of them. Lucy, however, kept standing.

"But in all," she said, "I'm doing OK."

"Are you homesick?"

"No. Not in the slightest. I haven't thought about any of my listings, I haven't thought about any of my clients, I haven't even thought about any of my competitors." She touched Jeff on the shoulder. "Are *you* homesick?"

"I am, I guess. I was looking at that garbage pile today, and all I could think of was being home and ordering at the drive-through and checking my e-mail and watching Jon Stewart."

"Now, I *do* miss Jon Stewart. Did you notice something about that garbage pile?"

"What?"

"All the plastic bags. Schuyler's crochet workshop could have gone for a month just from the plastic bags blowing around that pile, that intersection."

"I didn't notice."

"I think it shows what a great idea that workshop is. Have you seen the things they've been making? It's amazing. You'd never think they were made out of shopping bags."

Teddy stuck his head into the classroom.

"I think we're about ready to leave," he said.

"Let's huddle up for a team prayer and we can go our separate ways."

◆

Soon after Jeff and Axel arrived home, Elizabeth came in with a stack of neatly-folded laundry. After she left, Jeff and Axel looked at each other in amazement.

"I don't think my underwear was this white when it was on the shelf at Wal-Mart," said Jeff.

**EIGHT**
On, Comet! On, Cupid! On, Blixen!

"Today," said Teddy, "we will have some free time in the afternoon. I'm not sure I would have scheduled it this way – we haven't been having services in the evening, and so our schedule has been a little lighter than normal already. But Joe wants it this way; he's trying to take care of us. We have special plans for supper tonight. I know a little about it, but I'm not going to talk."

"This afternoon, you can either go downtown, or you can go to the Karen Blixen Museum. I will be going downtown. Dea will be going to the museum."

"What's the Karen Blixen Museum?" asked Axel.

"Have you ever seen the movie 'Out of Africa' with Meryl Streep and Robert Redford?" asked Dea. "That was based on an autobiographical book by a woman whose real name was Karen Blixen, although she used the pen name Isak Dinesen. She was from Denmark and she moved to Africa with her husband, but they divorced, and she ran their coffee plantation by herself. Some of the movie was filmed at her actual home, and now they've turned it into a museum about her life."

Jeff had read "Out of Africa" years earlier, and he loved the book but didn't care much for the movie. Denys Finch Hatton, the aviator played by Robert Redford in the movie, was ... *British*. In Jeff's imagination, he was a stiff-upper-lip British adventurer type. Redford, as far as Jeff was concerned, had been completely miscast. He would have looked silly attempting a British accent, and yet his portrayal was completely inaccurate without one.

"Count me in for the museum," said Jeff.

"Me, too," said Lucy.

They were, however, the only takers.

"Okay," said Dea. "George will take the three of us to the museum, and we've got a van to take the rest of you downtown. We'll meet at where we're going for dinner."

"But first," said Teddy, "we have a morning and a midday of ministry before us."

"On that note, do we have any concerns?" asked

Kate, who had been chairing the morning meeting.

"I was disappointed that no one came forward when we did street ministry yesterday," said Axel.

"Think back to the gospels," said Teddy. "Jesus sent out the disciples two by two, and he told them what to do if they were well received, and he told them what to do if they weren't well received. We've got to worry about whether we're doing what we should be doing to get the word out, but we have to leave the rest to God."

"Are we doing what we should be doing?" asked Axel.

"I think we are," said Teddy. "I think what we're doing here speaks more loudly than what we had to say out by the trash heap. That's not to take anything away from what we've done at the trash heap, or in our door-to-door visits, or during the worship services. But I suspect it's in our one-on-one interactions that we're making the most impact. We're empowering the people here at the church, and maybe after we leave they'll have the kind of impact that you're talking about."

"Speaking of the trash heap," asked Schuyler, "what happened to the guy that was yelling at us yesterday?"

Teddy fielded the question. "The church members just pulled him aside, Joe told me. He was kind of drunk, and they just pulled him out of the way and tried to calm him down."

"Okay," said Kate. "Anything else?"

"Jeff," said Teddy, "Dea and I need to see you for a second after the meeting."

◆

"You want me to what?"

"We want you to speak during the church service tomorrow morning," said Teddy.

"You mean, give my testimony?"

"No. Not exactly. Not in the way you did it for us last weekend. I want you to do kind of a devotional. Talk about how God has been present in your life and has comforted you in cases where you were frustrated or alone. Tie it in with Scripture. You don't have to be too wordy or too specific, but give them your heart."

"I don't know."

"You can do it," Teddy continued. "You have a giving heart, and you love God, and you know the Bible, and I think you can share that during the service tomorrow morning."

"All right. I'll try."

"Give it some thought," Dea said, "make an outline, but don't script it out too much. I want you to just talk to them."

"I'll try."

◆

The music at morning worship seemed especially ... African. The harmonies, the rhythms, the almost dream-like spirit. George, leading the singing, had to take off his suit jacket, and Elizabeth took off her shoes. Jeff raised his hands – something he never did in his plain old Methodist services back home – and swayed gently to the music. He couldn't understand the lyrics, which were in Swahili, but he trusted that they were something pleasing to God. He knew the music must be pleasing to God.

During the sermon, which was somewhat less rapturous, Jeff looked around and noticed Tony sitting a few pews away. Jeff spoke to him on the way out of the sanctuary; you could barely see the little burns from the spattering oil against his dark skin. But he seemed unaffected. He actually apologized to Jeff for having disrupted the class.

"No, no, no," said Jeff, "you have nothing to apologize for. I should have made sure there wasn't any moisture in the stock pot, and I shouldn't have left the classroom for so long and let the oil get as hot as it did. I am the one who should be apologizing to you."

"I am fine. Dea put something on the burn, and it does not hurt."

"Hopefully, we can get through class today without any injuries."

Tony laughed.

Teddy slipped in and stood in the corner, quietly, taking a few photos from time to time.

The class was greatly pleased to see that the soap had solidified inside the two wooden molds. Jeff

pointed out the score marks, which also drew
approval.

Given his druthers, he'd have waited to unmold
the soap, but he needed to use the molds again today,
and he didn't want to have to ask Axel – who was
hoping to get the water purification up and running
that day -- to make more. So he struck the side of one
wooden mold to loosen the soap's grip on the surface
of the table. He picked up the mold and carefully
pushed the bar out with his thumbs. He left
thumbprints but the soap was otherwise undamaged.
It was still a little soft, but not unworkably so.

He placed the first bar in the window sill and
unmolded the other. He also went back and
unmolded the hard soaps from the first day from
their plastic containers.

"Today, I'm not going to walk you through the
process. I want you to go ahead and start making the
soap yourselves."

Teddy smiled and nodded.

Tony stood up and was going to take charge of
measuring the lye water, but the goggles touched his
face right on the burns. He winced. He'd obviously
been lying when he said the burns didn't hurt. He
took the goggles off, handed them to Andrew and sat
down.

Jeff looked at him, sitting there, and felt terrible.

The students – at least, the ones who volunteered
– did a pretty good job of recreating the soap-making

process. He wasn't sure that everyone in the classroom had the same retention level, given some of the repeated questions from day to day.

Once the activity had settled down, Jeff opened it up for questions again.

"Can I use avocado to make soap?"

Apparently, this fellow had access to some locally-grown avocados and wanted to use them.

"Well, yes and no. There is a way to add a little bit of avocado to soap. We've talked about adding things like fragrances and colors to soap. You can also add small amounts of other things. There is a kind of soap called 'gardener's soap' which is made using brewed coffee instead of water and to which you add the coffee grounds. The coffee grounds give the soap a scrubby, abrasive feel that helps clean dirty hands."

Jeff wondered if Oscar was going to be able to translate "abrasive," much less "scrubby."

"There are recipes for soap which include a very small amount of avocado in order to moisturize your skin. But many of these recipes call for a preservative called benzoin which helps to keep the avocado from spoiling. I don't know if you would have a way to order benzoin here in Kenya or not, but I can leave a recipe.

"The other way to use avocado in soap would be to make soap from avocado oil. As I think I told you yesterday, there are various kinds of oils that can be used for soap-making. We have used beef tallow in this class because it is inexpensive. Avocado oil, at least back in the states, is much more expensive, but some people like it as part of a soap recipe.

"But I don't know how to extract oil from avocados. I think you may find that you can't get enough to make it worth your time from your home-grown avocados.

"The information I am leaving with the church shows how to adjust your soap recipe for various types of oils, including avocado oil, but that may be something you'll have to research on your own after I leave. The pastor has Internet access; perhaps he can help."

*Another case of me being blissfully unprepared.*

Just then, Jeff heard a cheer from out in the courtyard.

"What's that?" he asked Teddy.

"I think I know, but let's go see."

Jeff looked to make sure that the burner was turned off and he and Teddy stepped outside to see what was going on.

What was going on was that the chlorinator was working on a 50-gallon drum of water.

"We haven't had time to get this much through the filter system," Axel told Jeff. "So this isn't filtered water. But we are chlorinating it."

The McGuire Water Purifier, hooked up to a car battery, was producing chlorine gas, which was passing through a hose and bubbling up through the drum of water.

Axel was glowing like a 100-watt bulb, and his students were excited too. Jeff ducked back into his classroom and called his students out to see. The woman who had been stirring the soap just brought it with her and kept stirring.

"Dea needs to see this too," Axel told Teddy.

"Dea's a little under the weather."

"Oh, no – nothing serious, I hope."

"I don't think so. I think it's just, well, travelers' malaise. We have some Cipro samples from our doctor, and I think Dea's going to start taking them. She's lying down on a pew in the sanctuary."

It only took two minutes to chlorinate the barrel, and the unit was turned off. Axel used the common pool test kit which came with the unit to check the water's chlorine level.

"Perfect," he said. "Right now, there's more chlorine in here than would taste good to drink, but it's hard at work killing germs. Eventually, some of the chlorine will evaporate, but enough will stay behind to help keep the germs down."

Pastor Joe insisted on saying a prayer of thanks over the unit. After that, the soap-making students returned to their classroom.

The rest of the class was uneventful. Jeff insisted that Tony pour the soap into molds – by that time it was thick enough that spatters were less of a problem and safety goggles seemed less important.

Tony seemed grateful for the gesture.

There was sukuma wiki again for lunch, and Jeff tried to stomach it but was having trouble. Fortunately, he'd asked for small portions. He tried, bite by bite, to stomach it, but kept having gag reflex. And his guilt and discomfort just made him more self-conscious, which made the gag reflex worse. It grew so strong that he feared he was going to vomit.

He looked for a garbage can to scrape his plate into. But he'd already noticed that there were far, far fewer waste receptacles in Kenya than in the U.S. The only one he could see in the courtyard was a large plastic drum right next to where the food was being served, and he dared not scrape out his plate right next to the women who had cooked the food.

He slipped over to the outhouse, made sure no one was looking, spit what was in his mouth onto the plate and dumped the contents of the plate down the hole of the unlocked stall.

◆

"Dea has decided not to join you at the Blixen museum," Teddy told Jeff and Lucy. "She's still resting. I want you to go anyway – George will be driving – but please don't stop anywhere else or do anything else."

"Young man," mocked Axel in a deep, fatherly voice, "I want you to have my daughter back by midnight."

"I'm serious," said Teddy. "I know you're adults,

but Dea and I have responsibility for this trip, this team, and this is the first time we've ever send anybody off for something like this without one of the leaders being there."

"All right," moaned Jeff. "I promise we won't hunt for big game, or start a revolution, or burn down the Blixen museum."

The museum was located a brief drive outside the city. The neighborhood was pleasant and green – and seemed, from what little was visible from the highway, to be a relatively upper-class community. There was even a golf course not too far from the museum.

Lucy sat with George in the front seat of the car while Jeff was in the back. Lucy and Jeff talked about "Out of Africa," but George seemed to have little interest except to point out another time he'd driven some bank officials from abroad to the Blixen museum.

Jeff knew that either George or Elizabeth must be a reader – he'd seen a number of works by African authors on a bookshelf at their home. But it could be that, like "CSI," George thought of "Out of Africa" as just a story – and it wasn't really a story about the Kenya that George or his parents knew. It wasn't a story about Kenya so much as it was a story about a mzungu in Kenya.

"I think seeing Africa in that movie is part of what made me want so badly to see it in person," said

Lucy.

"I just couldn't get over Redford," said Jeff. "Denys Finch Hatton was as British as they come. He's like Lawrence of Arabia ... or Doctor Who."

"'He's like Lawrence of Arabia, or Doctor Who.'" Lucy turned around in the seat to look at Jeff. "Let's think about that, for a second."

"On the one hand, I'm being mocked ... but on the other hand, you at least know who Doctor Who is."

"Well, I'd rather have Robert Redford than, I don't know, Hugh Grant any day of the week," said Lucy.

"Hugh Grant is even less like Denys Finch-Hatton than Robert Redford."

"I'm sorry, George," said Lucy. "We haven't really included you in the conversation."

"It is no problem."

Jeff leaned forward. "How much farther is it?"

"Just up here."

The house where Karen Blixen held court, listening to the problems and disputes of her African employees and neighbors, is both modest and beautiful, or at least Jeff thought it was beautiful.

"I can just imagine Baroness Blixen strolling the grounds," said Jeff.

"And Robert Redford," said Lucy, a twinkle in her green eyes.

"No, not Robert Redford."

*Maybe that's my problem*, Jeff thought. *Maybe I'm*

*Hugh Grant, and what she's looking for is Bob Redford.*

*Heck, I'm not even Hugh Grant. I'm more like that guy who plays Hagrid in the Harry Potter movies.*

They saw the millstone table where Karen Blixen sat at the rear of the house and smoked and looked at the clouds as the rolled across the Ngong Hills.

The interior of the house has been restored, as much as possible, to look the way it looked when Karen Blixen lived there. There were various photos and explanations hanging on the corridor walls and other places around the house. A small museum store has been built onto one end of the house.

Jeff pictured Karen sitting at her desk poring over the declining fortunes of her coffee plantation. But that reminded him of his own finances, and he tried to put the image out of his mind.

He doubted Mr. Redford was in debt, now or when he was starring in "Out of Africa."

"This is so beautiful," Lucy said. She was staring off into the hills. Jeff stared at the back of her neck and the curve of her back.

Jeff went into the bookstore. He already had a dog-eared copy of "Out of Africa" in his book bag, but he bought another one – just to say that he'd bought it at her home – as well as a small souvenir book with photos of and information about the home.

He came out of the bookshop and didn't see Lucy anywhere. Around the back, he saw her sitting at the millstone table.

"Are you thinking of buying the place," Jeff asked, "or do you want it as a listing?"

"I was just play acting," said Lucy. "I was wondering what it would be like to be her, living here."

She noticed Jeff's books.

"Is that 'Out of Africa'?" she asked.

"It is." he opened the book to a page two-thirds of the way through.

"Pride," he read to Lucy, "is faith in the idea that God had, when he made us."

"I like that."

"It really is a terrific book. I mean, there are passages in the book ...." He sought for the right words. "Reading it now, in the 21$^{st}$ Century, Karen Blixen can seem a little condescending. She was a baroness, after all. But for her time, she was compassionate, and enlightened, and just such a wonderful observer. Way ahead of her time. And she could write so beautifully."

"Or the translator could. Wasn't she Danish?"

"She was, but she wrote in English. Then she went back and translated each book into Danish. That makes it even more amazing."

"And Denys was British, as you keep telling me."

"I never realized you were actually listening."

"You'd be surprised."

"Anyway, when Hemingway got the Nobel Prize in 1954, he said in an interview afterward that he'd have been happier if it had gone to Karen."

"Wow."

George had remained with the car the whole time. Jeff had offered to pay the 200 shillings it cost to tour the museum, but George wasn't interested. Jeff hoped he hadn't insulted George by offering to pay for the ticket.

The ride back to Nairobi was strangely quiet. Jeff thought about the movie, and its over-romanticized notions of Karen Blixen wanting to possess the free spirit Robert Red – er, Denys Finch Hatton. As far as Hollywood was concerned, the story of Karen Blixen was largely one of unrequited love, or at least unrequited commitment.

Jeff liked the book better.

◆

George turned off next to Uchumi, a large supermarket on what appeared to be the outskirts of town – Jeff thought, but wasn't sure, that it was on the way to the airport. There was a sign that read "CARNIVORE" pointing down the little side road. After a ways, there was a guard shack, and the guard checked a list and let George and his passengers in.

"Do you think the others are already here?" asked Lucy.

"I think we are probably early," said George.

Carnivore was, indeed, the name of the restaurant. The stucco exterior of the building looked to Jeff like something out of a theme park. There was an entrance to the restaurant, complete with a fiberglass crocodile; an entrance to a bar next door; and even a little souvenir shop.

The smell, however, was delicious – smoky and inviting, like a barbecue joint. It wasn't at all like the dirty smoky smell that Jeff had begun to associate with the slums.

"I don't know if I can make it until the others get here," said Lucy.

"Me either. I didn't really eat lunch today."

"I thought the sukuma wiki was good."

"I'm sure it was. I'm just having problems – er, I just didn't care for it."

"Okay."

Just then, the van pulled in to the parking lot, followed by Joe and Helen's car. As the group disembarked, they, too, seemed shocked and delighted by the experience.

"How was the museum?" Schuyler asked Jeff.

"It was a great experience. It's not often you get to see the setting for one of your favorite books in that kind of detail."

"Be glad your favorite book isn't 'The Wizard of Oz.'"

"What about downtown?"

"It was incredible. We went to the memorial where they blew up the U.S. Embassy. I cried."

The group had reservations and was swiftly admitted to the restaurant. There was a huge open pit, visible as you entered, with huge pieces of meat on skewers cooking over it.

They were seated at two long tables placed end-to-end. In addition to the Americans, and George, there was Elizabeth, Oscar, and Joe and Helen. Dea was not with the group; Oscar's wife Susan had stayed home with her. Teddy told Lucy and Jeff that Dea was doing fine and would be back up and around the next day.

"You didn't bring Sally?" Jeff asked Elizabeth.

"No," she answered, without explanation. This was apparently a night out for grownups.

"Foreign visitors like this place," said Joe to the group.

"Your meal is paid for," added Teddy, "as part of our trip budget. Hot tea and coffee are included in the price. If you want a soft drink or a bottled water, we'll need you to cover that yourself."

Jeff ordered a Stoney Tangawizi, drawing curious looks from all of the other Americans except Axel (who had tasted a swig of Jeff's at the convenience store and didn't like it).

The waiters brought out what they called farmer's soup, with lentils and other vegetables, and it wasn't bad. Meanwhile, they brought out little lazy-suzan towers and placed one on each table. Each tower had a little plastic flag on top.

"When we are through eating," said Joe, smiling, "we will take the flags down and surrender."

A cast-iron plate was placed in front of each diner.

"This is actually a churrascaria ," Teddy whispered to Jeff, who was seated next to him. "It's not African at all – it's South American, Brazilian, except for the choice of protein."

"Choice of protein?" Jeff asked.

The waiter explained the protein choices, by listing which of the sauces on the lazy susan went with each. There would be beef, chicken, lamb, pork, sausages, chicken livers, ostrich, gazelle meatballs and crocodile.

Servers began making the rounds of the table. They would ask if the diner wanted what they were serving ("Lamb?"), plop the skewer down on the middle of the diner's cast iron plate and carve off a slice of meat, or push off a chicken piece or meatball from the bottom of the skewer.

The familiar meats were all wonderful, Jeff thought, and he enjoyed the ostrich as well. He didn't like the crocodile, which had a fishy taste and a texture like chicken, or the gazelle meatballs. He didn't try the chicken livers or the sausages.

When everyone was sated, the flags were taken down and the servers stopped coming. But the waiter returned to offer a choice of small desserts – most of the Americans picked the small dish of ice cream.

"I couldn't eat another bite," said Schuyler after wolfing down her ice cream.

That was the consensus of the group, as they wobbled back out to the vehicles. The van driver, who had waited patiently during the meal, took Oscar and Teddy home; Joe, Helen and the ladies packed their way into Joe's car. George, Axel and Jeff climbed into George's car.

"Did you enjoy Carnivore?" George asked.

"I'll say we did," said Axel.

Once they were on the road, Axel in the front seat turned to Jeff in the back seat expectantly.

"So?"

"So, what?"

"How did it go with Lucy today?"

"Honestly, Axel, I'm not sure I know."

## NINE
### My Other Car is a Matatu

Jeff, Axel, Elizabeth, George and Sally were seated in the car Thursday morning, ready to go to the church.

Nothing was happening. George was turning the key to no effect.

"The car won't go," said Sally, mournfully.

"Pop the hood," said Axel, "and let me take a look at it."

The problem appeared to be the alternator, and the battery had totally drained overnight.

"We will take a matatu," said George.

Axel wanted to keep working.

"Axel," said Jeff, "I'm supposed to be speaking at

worship this morning. And you're supposed to be purifying water."

They locked up the car, and the five of them walked down the street and to the security gate for the housing development.

George started hailing the white-and-yellow vans. Two of them were full, but the third one stopped. George conversed with the driver in Swahili, and the group packed aboard.

There was not enough room for everyone to sit. The driver gestured for Jeff to sit in the front passenger seat. Elizabeth and the baby sat down, and one of the younger Kenyans tried to offer his seat to Axel, but Axel turned it down and he and George remained hunched over in the gap behind the driver's seat.

The matatu swerved and dodged through Nairobi traffic, with Jeff and Axel trying to keep their balance. It stopped a few times to take on or drop off passengers, before heading down the side streets towards the church.

As they got out, Axel straightened up and stretched, and Jeff walked over to him and pointed to the front passenger-side tire, which was so badly frayed that there was little tread left.

"Hey," said Axel, grinning. "God is my co-pilot."

◆

Dea was at the morning meeting, looking a little weary but otherwise well.

"I don't know what happened," she said. "It just shows you have to be careful about everything you eat and drink on one of these trips. It's just embarrassing for it to happen to me after everything Teddy and I have said to you about it."

"Poetic justice," said Teddy.

"Speaking of food and drink," said Schuyler, who was chairing the morning meeting, "does anyone have any thoughts about Carnivore last night?"

"I really enjoyed it while I was there," said Kate, "but when I was lying in bed last night it bothered me."

"Bothered your stomach?" Jeff asked. "Like Dea?"

"Ha, ha. No, I mean it bothered me, because here we are dealing with people who are living in such poverty, and then we go, right in the middle of it all, to this place that's done up like the Rainforest Café, or Disneyland, or what have you, and we stuff our faces with food that the people at the church couldn't afford if they saved up for six months."

"Do others feel that way?" asked Schuyler. "Or do you think of last night as just a little reward for our hard work?"

"I had the same kind of thoughts," said Jeff. "I was sitting there last night thinking of people back home who I wanted to regale with stories about the world traveler eating gazelle meatballs. But then I realized I don't want to be a tourist with stories to tell.

When I go home, I want to tell them about what we're doing here, and I don't want to get the stories confused."

"That's interesting," said Teddy. "Because, you know, our debrief is going to be at a safari park. I guarantee you, there will be things you'll see and experience at the safari park that you will want to talk about back home. I think you're right, Jeff, that you don't want to be only a tourist with snapshots, but I also think part of telling people about Africa is telling people about, well, Africa. And if we're interested in building up Africa's economy, it's good to encourage people to come here as tourists, just as we encourage people to come here as missionaries. But we're getting ahead of ourselves. We will talk more during debrief about how to tell your story when you get home.

"But I also think Kate has a good point, and it's one we'll also be talking about during debrief. How does what we see here relate to how we live our lives – whether it's what we eat, or what we buy, or what have you?

"Let's not get too far ahead of ourselves, but let's be prepared to talk about that question a little bit when we get to Masai Mara."

"In the meantime," said Schuyler, "we've got quite a bit to do here. We've had some requests for a women's seminar, talking about some health issues and concerns. So the women of the church will meet in the sanctuary with me and Dea. We'll have a men's meeting at the same time in one of the Sunday school rooms, which Teddy will lead, and Kate and Lucy will lead the kids in some outdoor games in the courtyard, some things she hasn't been able to do during her morning workshops.

"Axel, I understand, is going to go home with George and try to work on the car. Jeff, you can sit in with Teddy or you can play with the kids."

"Wherever I'm needed," said Jeff.

"I have no idea what we're going to be talking about," said Teddy. "It's the women's workshop that was specifically requested, so I'm still trying to come up with some content."

"I'll sit in with you to start out with," said Jeff, "but if it looks like I'm not needed I'll slip out and play with the kids."

"Deal."

◆

"Brother Teddy will preach to us today," said Joe, "but first, Brother Jeff will speak to us."

Jeff stepped to the front of the sanctuary.

"Bwana asifiwe!" The congregation responded in kind.

"My name is Jeff Doerman, and I come from Tennessee, in the United States. I guess you knew that." Laughter followed translation.

"I became a Christian as a young child. But we are all young in Christ at first.

"Some people, some well-known preachers in the

United States, and I know that they have even visited here in Kenya, would have you believe that when you become a Christian, all of your problems go away and God showers you with wealth.

"But that's not exactly what we see in the Bible. We see men in the Bible who were persecuted, even executed, for the sake of what they believed. God didn't take those problems away. In the book of Acts, we see that Stephen was stoned for being a follower of Christ."

He read the story of Stephen from Acts.

"What God promises us is that he will be with us through our problems, that he will lighten our burden as long as we are willing to give up our burden and trust in him. Just as Stephen saw a vision of Jesus at his time of crisis, God will be with us through our struggles.

"This week, in your community, I saw a woman who had a terrible disease. I prayed for her. I do not know how God will answer that prayer. Perhaps God will answer that prayer with comfort, by giving that woman the knowledge of God's presence as she bears this terrible hardship. Perhaps God will answer that prayer with a miracle, an unexpected recovery. I never want to be so cold-hearted that I ignore the ways in which God acts unexpectedly. Perhaps God will answer that prayer through you. Perhaps you will be God's hands and feet in giving comfort to those who are in suffering and need.

"I must admit to you, I spend far too much time worrying about problems that aren't really problems. I worry about problems that are mostly up here" -- he tapped his temple.

"Sometimes, when we think that God is not answering my prayer, it's because I'm worried about these silly little problems and I fail to see how he's got his arms around me, getting me through the big problems in my life.

"The problems we face in America are quite different from what you face here in Kibera. Perhaps we have no right to speak to you of God's love and God's blessings, because too often we in America have hoarded those blessings.

"But this week, I hope, and I believe, God is teaching me, about my problems, and about my priorities, and about my possibilities if I am obedient to him. 1 John 2, 5 through 7, says that if we are obedient to God, we will be made complete in him. Sometimes I don't feel complete, but I'm moving in that direction.

"Thank you." He sat down.

"No, no, Brother Jeff, please come back," said Pastor Joe. "You have spoken beautifully about prayer. We want you to pray for us now. Are there any who are in need of prayer?"

About eight or ten people came forward. The worship team got back up and began leading the congregation in song. Jeff decided that they were asking him to pray for each person, individually.

The first person was a young woman. Jeff tried to ask her what she needed prayer for. The music had become so loud that he could not understand much of her heavily-accented response, but he did make out "to feed my children." He prayed for food, and provision.

The next person, an old man missing half of his teeth, Jeff couldn't understand at all. He prayed a general prayer of God's blessing.

Jeff found himself raising his voice to compete with the music – but he seemed to also become more fervent with each prayer, caught up in the emotion of the moment. He had to laugh at himself a little.

*All I need now*, he thought, *is a big-haired wife and a Bible college named after me.*

He finished praying for each of the people, and then led a general prayer, and sat down.

After the service, he rushed up to Helen and handed her his journal, open to a blank page.

"Can you write down the names of the people I prayed for? I'd like to keep them in prayer."

"God bless you, Jeff."

While he was waiting for Helen to write the names, Dea came up and gave him a big hug.

"I knew you would be a blessing. No, I said that wrong – I know you are a blessing."

◆

"Can soap be made without the hydroxide?"

"Well," said Jeff, "you must have something like sodium hydroxide. Now, in the old days, they got a chemical much like sodium hydroxide from ashes. In fact, the notebook of information that I will leave with the church has information about how to do that. You may want to try it some time, to make soap for your own personal use. But I am afraid that it would not be something you would want to do for soap that you would sell. It would be unattractive and not like the commercial product.

"Also, it is harder to measure the proper amount and be sure that your soap is properly balanced between hydroxide and fat, so that all of the hydroxide becomes soap.

"Actually, the chlorination machine that Axel is using produces a small amount of sodium hydroxide water, and that can be used for making soap – but, again, the trick is measuring it so that you know how much of it to use."

"What happens," asked Andrew, "if you use the wrong amount of hydroxide?"

"Well, if you use too much hydroxide and not enough fat, your soap will be dry, and crumbly, and it would irritate the skin if you tried to use it. If you used too much fat and not enough hydroxide, your soap will be soft and squishy and will leave your skin feeling oily.

"The good news is that if you have a batch that turns out badly, you do not have to throw it away.

Just as we have been grating soap to melt it down and add fragrances and colors to it, we can grate down badly-made soap and fix it, by adding a little bit more hydroxide water or a little more fat depending on which you need. The soap can then be poured back into molds."

"Will you be giving us certificates for this course?"

Jeff started to answer, but Oscar stepped in. It was the fourth straight day the question had been asked, and after hearing Jeff answer it on Tuesday and Wednesday Oscar knew the answer well enough to state it himself, in Swahili, instead of translating it. Oscar and the man asking the question engaged in a conversation in Swahili, and a couple of other class members jumped in, and Jeff shrugged and sat down until they finished hashing out the point.

"I told him he should not ask a question that had been asked before," said Oscar.

"I appreciate that, but I don't want to discourage anyone from asking any kind of question."

Jeff was actually enjoying the questions and answers – it made him feel like everyone was engaged and planning to follow up on the craft once he had gone.

Dea had wanted Jeff, Lucy and Schuyler to talk some about how to market the cottage industry products. But Jeff wasn't exactly sure where to begin. The issue with the shape of the bars had indicated that he really didn't know that much about the Kenyan market.

"I think that the church is planning to start a cooperative which will enable you to get started producing your products together, and that will allow you to share some information and supplies like sodium hydroxide.

"But the goal, of course, is to sell your products. Do you know how to go about that?"

"We will need a certificate," said the man who had asked the question earlier. Oscar started to respond but Jeff held up a hand and stopped him.

"Perhaps that will be something that the cooperative can address. I do not think I will be able to help you with that this week.

"Now ... we will need to do a presentation tomorrow for the group explaining what we have learned. I would like to have a different person explain each stage of the process. Who would like to talk about the basics of soapmaking?"

◆

Jeff, in flagrant violation of Dea's instructions, spent the lunch period hidden in the office, sipping on a Coke and avoiding whatever they were having for lunch.

"I thought I'd find you here," said Schuyler. She handed him a bag of potato chips.

"Where did you get these?"

"Yesterday, downtown. I figured you might need

them."

"Bless you, my child."

The chips were Kenya-made and came in a clear plastic bag instead of the silvery laminate favored back in the states. But they tasted like normal potato chips, and as far as Jeff was concerned they were wonderful.

"How was your workshop this morning?" Jeff asked.

"It was great. We've had a wonderful time, talking and getting to know each other. And they've gotten a good start on their projects, especially the handbags."

"I'm glad to hear it. I don't guess I've made exactly that kind of emotional connection with my students. But I think it's been productive, or at least I hope it has."

"I'm sure it has."

Jeff looked for a place to throw his potato chip wrapper, and, as usual, couldn't find one. He stuffed it into his pocket.

"Let me ask you, Schuyler: How does this week compare to the trips you've been on before?"

"Hard comparison. Both of my other trips were to Latin America, and one of them was a Methodist trip to Mexico where we were spending the night in Texas and driving over the border every day. This is a whole different thing. It's nice being able to talk directly to people – I could never do that in Nicaragua or Mexico, because very few people spoke much English. But there are other points where I'm feeling a lot more culture shock here than I felt over there."

"I wish people wouldn't be so deferential. I wish I knew better ways to get around that without hurting people's feelings."

"I feel the same way."

"There are times when I feel kind of helpless. What are we really doing to change this culture, this situation? Maybe we're all fooling ourselves this week if we think we're doing any good."

"Jeff, *nobody's* going to change a culture, any culture, on a two-week mission trip. But that doesn't mean you don't go on mission trips. You just have to be patient, and stick to your knitting, and trust that maybe God will do something to bless your efforts.

"Maybe you're not here to change them. Maybe you're here to change Jeff Doerman."

"If I could change, I'd be out there with a plate of food."

"You don't think you've changed *this week*?"

◆

Some of the men had drifted away during lunch, and the crowd for the men's seminar in the classroom was much smaller than the one for the women's seminar in the sanctuary.

"We're here to talk," said Teddy. "We, as brothers in Christ, have much that we can learn from each other. I want you all to speak freely, and I want all of us to treat each other with respect in this room."

"I have a question," said an elderly gentleman in the back of the room."

"Wonderful."

"If a man who is not a Christian has two wives, and then he becomes a Christian, what should he do about them?"

"Wow," said Teddy.

"I think they need me in the children's workshop," said Jeff.

◆

Kate and Lucy were trying to teach the younger children how to play "Duck, Duck, Goose." There were a few of the older children, including the two younger orphans, Mwai and Geoffrey, who had lost interest and were hanging around at the perimeter of things. (Guy had the three older orphans in the men's workshop.)

Jeff walked over to them. He sat on a bench over at the edge of the courtyard and reached into his backpack, pulling out the three-ring binder in which a lot of his training materials and other official documents were kept. He flipped through the notebook and found a few pages from pre-field orientation that he didn't think he'd need any more. Without saying a word, he took one of them and folded it into a paper airplane. The first airplane was the normal, spiky kind of paper airplane that every child learns to make. He looked the children in the eye, winked, and then threw it.

The children rushed to pick up the airplane and bring it back, and Jeff showed one of them how to throw it. As the children played with the airplane, Jeff started folding a different design, a flat body shaped like home plate with the point cut off, which tended to fly in acrobatic loops. It was a little complicated to fold, and he had to think back a bit, but it came to him.

The children were delighted with the two airplanes and started playing with them. Jeff, meanwhile, went over and sat in the circle for "Duck, Duck, Goose."

At one point, after chasing someone around the circle, Jeff found himself sitting right next to Lucy.

"Are you OK?" she asked.

"Just a little out of breath," said Jeff. *On account of being a fat slob.*

"Well, we're at high altitude here. Take care of yourself."

"You, too," Jeff said. You've been pushing yourself hard this week."

After the game, Kate got ready to teach the kids a song, and Jeff walked over to pull the older ones back into the group. They handed his paper airplanes back to him as if they were precious possessions.

"No," Jeff said. "You can keep those. Just put them down right now and come over here with the rest of the group."

Later, Kate asked Jeff to read a story to the group. Jeff thought he was nicely theatrical about things, and the kids, especially the younger ones, seemed to enjoy it. Sally came up and paid special attention to him after the story. He slipped her a piece of candy on the sly.

After the women's and men's workshops broke up, Lucy chatted with one of the mothers while Jeff made sure that two of the children who had been playing with the paper airplanes took them home, and he even made another airplane for one of the other children. Kate watched him.

"We did craft projects earlier in the week," she said, "with some construction paper and popsicle sticks I'd brought from the States. When we broke for lunch, some of the parents brought the craft projects back to me. It never occurred to them that the kids would be allowed to keep them."

"I guess paper isn't something you waste here."

"Paper airplanes are never a waste," said Kate. "You're good with kids."

"I have nieces and nephews. I also know my limitations, and I don't try too hard."

"Well, thanks for helping today."

"Thanks for giving me an excuse."

Jeff saw Teddy and walked over to him.

"I didn't realize they had polygamy in Kenya."

"Jeff, I have to admit something to you. I had read something about it in passing, but I thought it was more prevalent in the rural areas. Well, I guess it *is* more prevalent in the rural areas. But the little old man came here from somewhere in southwestern Kenya."

"What did you tell him?"

"I told him we did not have polygamy in the states, and so it wasn't something I felt qualified to speak about. I told him he should speak to Pastor Joe."

"I'm sorry I bailed on you."

"You went where you were needed. From what I could see, you were having a good time with the kids."

"I figured a lot of the questions were going to be marriage-related anyway."

"Many of them were. And some of them were cultural things that it was hard for me to understand from their perspective. The women were talking more about health issues, and you can look those up in a book. I wish Pastor Joe had been in there with us, but he had business in the city. I think he and Axel were buying parts for George's car."

"How am I getting home tonight, by the way?"

"I think Joe will be back here and will take you home. We may have to take a couple of trips to get everyone where they need to go."

"How's Dea doing?"

"She's doing better. I think the antibiotic is working."

"Glad to hear it. Has Joe been happy with the way things have turned out so far?"

"I think he is. And he's been getting good feedback on the soapmaking workshop."

"Well, I hope so. I feel like all I've done is given them a very cursory introduction. I should have worked up more content, and I should have tried to figure out some color and scent options they could use here."

"You did what you could in the time you had, Jeff. From what I could see when I looked in on you, you were doing a great job. You were right to keep things simple. Maybe they have some more to learn before they can make a profit, but this is only going to work if they take it from here, and that may mean teaching themselves. And I think Joe is committed to following up with them. I know you're leaving some background information – do you have links to some web sites?"

"I do."

"Joe has Internet access, of course – but you'd be surprised that there are web cafés not far from here where people can look things up."

Just then, Joe came through the gate into the compound.

"Pastor!" called out Teddy.

"Brother Teddy!"

"Did Axel get George's car up and running again?"

"He is still working on it. I do not think it will take him long. I will take Lucy, Schuyler and Kate home. Helen will stay here with Jeff, Elizabeth and Sally. I will come back for them."

"We can take a matatu if that would be simpler," said Jeff. "I don't mind."

"He's becoming a Kenyan already," laughed Joe.

When it was time to leave, Helen gathered Jeff, Elizabeth and Sally and headed out to the main road. Just as Joe turned his car onto the highway, Helen extended her hand – and a matatu stopped, immediately, in front of them.

"What Mama Church wants, Mama Church gets," said Jeff, and Helen and Elizabeth laughed heartily.

## TEN
### Fishing for compliments

The matatu dropped Jeff, Elizabeth and Sally off at the gate to the housing development, and Elizabeth spoke to the guard, who opened the gate and let them in.

As they rounded the corner, they saw the car parked in front of the house with a beaming Axel watching the motor run.

"You did it!" Jeff said.

"I did. Once we found the parts, and the tools. We ended up getting a new battery, too."

He slammed the hood shut and picked up Sally, who had run directly to him.

"How'd it go this afternoon at the church?"

"It was fun. You'd have had fun with the kids."

"Count on it."

◆

Dinner was spaghetti with a meatless tomato sauce. It was strangely comforting, and yet somehow different.

After dinner, Jeff and Axel and George and Elizabeth sat down in the living room. Axel turned on the TV, and there was soccer coverage.

"Tell me about where you live back in the states," George said to Jeff.

"Well, it's a small town – much smaller than Nairobi. It's about 60 miles – how many kilometers would that be? A little less than 100. A little less than 100 kilometers from a city called Nashville."

"The town where you live – are people farmers?"

"We have some farms in my area – but fewer than there used to be. Many of them are being sold and turned into housing."

"You said you work at a factory that makes pencils. Is that what do people do for a living?"

"Well, we have factories, but we also have shops, and offices, and banks, and some people drive into other counties to work. People think much less about driving to work or shop than they do here."

"I have heard that."

"I know you work at a bank – how have you been able to be with us this week?"

"I have taken days off. I knew this was important

to the church."

"I had to worry about whether I had enough vacation days to come here."

"I am glad you and Axel came. It has been good for the church, and I think the workshops will be quite successful."

"I hope so."

"Do you make much soap at home?" asked Elizabeth.

"I didn't – I had to learn how in order to come here and teach it. But I had good teachers. And I enjoy it – I plan to make it more often. If I come back here again, perhaps I'll have some new ideas and recipes to share."

"Would you like to come back?" asked George.

"I would. You have all made us feel so welcome, and I hope we have been good guests."

"It's been a great week," said Axel.

"Do you enjoy football?" George asked Axel.

"Football?" Axel realized that George was referring to the soccer game they were watching. "Oh, yes, football. I don't follow it that closely back in the states, but maybe I should. It's a fun game."

"I was quite good when I was younger."

"I'd like to have seen that."

They brought out Jenga and played it a few times, and then let Sally knock down the tower a few times.

Later, after Sally had gone to bed, they watched the news on television. At one point, Axel had excused himself to go to the restroom and George had gone to take a dirty glass to the kitchen. Elizabeth walked over to where Jeff was.

"Jeff," she said, "did you know that Lucy isn't married either?"

"I think she mentioned it, yes."

"Oh."

◆

Lying in bed, Jeff thought about Elizabeth's remark. Elizabeth had no doubt meant to be encouraging, but Jeff wondered if Lucy's status was significant in a different way.

*Maybe I wouldn't be attracted to her in real life. Maybe I'm homesick, here on the other side of the world, and she's someone to cling to. She and Kate are the only single members of the team, and Kate's a child, so I'm naturally drawn to Lucy. Maybe we have no real basis for any sort of relationship, and when we get back to the States we'd find out we really didn't care all that much for each other.*

*And maybe I should quit worrying and get to sleep.*

◆

"We will have morning worship," said Teddy, "and then you'll have some time with your workshops – but remember, as we told you earlier, it won't be the full period. Then we'll have a celebration ceremony and recognize each of the workshops."

"There's going to be trouble," said Jeff, "when we don't give out certificates."

Teddy smiled. "No doubt. If there's any trouble, Schuyler has promised to protect me."

"Pending a better offer from someone else," said Schuyler.

"After lunch, we – along with some of the church leaders – will spend some time in the sanctuary running through the plans for the pastoral leadership seminar tomorrow. Dea and I will be teaching it, of course, but we'll need all the rest of you in support roles, and we may call on you for things like skits."

"Don't forget," Dea said, "this morning will be your last chance to connect with your workshop students. Don't forget to have some kind of closure."

◆

Andrew had brought a bottle of perfume to soapmaking class and wanted to try rebatching some soap and scenting it. There wouldn't be time to make soap from scratch, but rebatching would probably work, so Andrew assented. But they'd run out of Jeff's sample soaps. So Jeff decided to use the individual bars they had poured during the first class on Monday.

"They may still be alkaline, but I'm guessing the alkalinity has gone down enough that they won't kill the scent. We'll rebatch with them – but let's wear gloves when we grate the soap just in case it's alkaline enough to irritate the skin."

At that point, Tony produced a little bag of green powder.

"This is a dye," he said. "A friend of mine says it is safe to use for coloring soap."

"Fine. Let's try a little of it."

They grated and melted down the soap and stirred in a few drops of the perfume and a light sprinkle of the dye. Jeff had warned them to use just a sprinkle, not knowing the dye's intensity, and because soap is supposed to have pastel hues.

Because the soap had not completely melted – it still had a cottage-cheese texture – the resulting color was green with white speckles. But it wasn't unattractive.

"We will leave these bars at the church. Please remember that they aren't to be used until they have cured. I'm also leaving the scale, these pots and the other things we've been using this week.

"I want to thank all of you for being here this week. It has been a good experience for me, and I hope it has been helpful for you. Pastor Joe, I'm sure, will have more to say to you in the weeks to come about how to set up a cooperative here at the church that will let you sell your products."

He led the group in a closing prayer and began to pick up the supplies. Several people thanked him for the workshop as they filed out of the room.

"Brother Jeff?" asked Andrew.

"Yes, Andrew, what is it?"

"May I have your e-mail address?"

"Certainly." Jeff wrote it on a page of his journal

and handed it to Andrew.

It was odd to think about Andrew – whose tiny, mud-walled shack Jeff had visited on Monday – having e-mail, but he knew from what Teddy and Dea had said that some of the church members had access to cyber-cafés or other computers. He wondered if Andrew was going to e-mail him asking for money, as Dea had warned earlier in the week. If that happened, he hoped he would be able to handle the situation gracefully.

Tony was also still in the room.

"How is your face doing, Tony?"

"It is fine. I am doing fine. I want to thank you for teaching us to make soap this week."

◆

Church members brought benches from the sanctuary out into the courtyard, which is where the workshop presentations were planned.

The water system, however, was located in a corner and didn't lend itself to a big group demonstration during the program, so before everyone sat down, Axel and several of his students showed anyone who was interested how the system worked.

"The filter system won't be completely effective for a couple of weeks," said Axel. "There is a bio-sand filter that will form in the top two inches of the sand barrel – good bacteria that will help to fight bad bacteria. But even as it is, it's a vast improvement over what they had before, and we have three or four different people from the church who have been trained to use the chlorinator."

The group then sat down for the presentations. Schuyler and her students went first. They showed some impressive-looking crocheted creations and talked about what other projects could be attempted.

Lucy and her candle-making workshop were next. Lucy had shown various ways to add colors and unusual shapes to candles, and the workshop members appeared quite pleased at the variety and spoke about how they would be able to sell the candles at a profit.

Jeff had Andrew talk about the soap-making process and Tony talk about the rebatching process. Samples were passed around for the congregation to examine.

Dea and Pastor Joe both spoke about the importance of the cottage industry workshops to the future.

"I wish we had time to talk more about packaging, pricing and marketing our products," Dea said. "That may be a project for a future trip."

Joe spoke about how, if the church could build a second floor onto the classroom building, there would be room for the projects to be done in a cooperative.

"This will benefit both the people and the church," he said.

Jeff wondered whether this meant that the church

would be taking a percentage of the profits, and whether that was a good thing. But he decided it would be cynical to dwell on it; he would ask Teddy and Dea later what they knew about Pastor Joe's intentions.

Kate then brought her kids up. They sang a song and then showed off some of their craft projects.

After that, Pastor Joe asked the team to gather in front of the crowd. Small paper bags were brought out for each one.

"We have a souvenir of Africa for each of you," he said. "We want you to know how much we appreciate you as brothers and sisters in Christ."

Inside each bag were a soapstone candle holder, a soapstone soap dish, a soapstone mug and a little beaded key ring with the word "Kenya." Jeff wondered if the key ring was made at the place they had seen in the slums.

"The candle-holder is for candles," said Pastor Joe. "The soap dish is for soap, the mug is for water and the beads – well, it is not crochet, but perhaps it looks a little like crochet."

"It's all beautiful," said Teddy. "We thank you very much."

◆

Jeff decided he would try to eat lunch with the crowd. It was, unfortunately, sukuma wiki. With great resolve, he managed to swallow two bites before gagging on the third. He was trying not to let

Tony or Oscar or Elizabeth see that he was gagging, which made it even worse. He ate the ugali instead – it was bland and unappetizing, especially with his stomach still turning flips, but he was able to get it down by taking swigs of Stoney Tangawizi after each bite. Helen had made sure a bottle of the Stoney Tangawizi was in the icebox and that everyone knew it was for Jeff.

After lunch, Teddy and Dea had to talk to Joe and Helen about travel arrangements, and so the meeting about the leadership workshop was postponed for a bit. Jeff found Schuyler sitting in the courtyard.

"How are you making it?" he asked.

"Good, I think."

"Thank you for talking me into this. This has been a great thing for me."

"I'm glad to know that. I've wondered, for obvious reasons, whether or not I should have made the trip, but that makes me feel better, it really does."

"Taking the trip wouldn't have changed anything. He obviously had his mind made up before the trip."

"Maybe."

"I shouldn't have said that. It's none of my business. But I'm glad you're here, and I think God has used you here, and I can't imagine you not being here."

"I love you, Jeff."

"I love you, Schuyler."

"Is there something going on between you and Lucy, by the way?"

"Not ... not that I know of. I guess I have a little bit of a trip crush, but I don't think she's interested, and this probably isn't the time or the place."

"'Trip crush.' Did you make that up yourself?"

"I guess I did."

"Well, don't count yourself out. Have you said anything to her?"

"Not really."

"Well, you moron, how do you know she's not interested?"

"She ... uh ... she prefers Robert Redford."

Schuyler rolled her eyes.

◆

During the planning meeting for the leadership workshop, various roles were assigned. The team would help with sign-in, would facilitate things for Teddy and Dea, and so on. Lucy, who had some calligraphy skills, offered to write the names of the participating pastors on certificates.

"*Now* we have certificates," whined Jeff, throwing up his hands in mock annoyance.

"This is more of a formalized course," said Teddy. Jeff wasn't sure if he didn't quite catch the playful nature of the joke or if he was pretending not to because of the Kenyans in the room. Perhaps the Kenyans would take offense or think Jeff had been trying to mock them.

Dea asked Kate and Jeff to help with an exercise called "oogley." This was a demonstration which accompanied a part of the training about having to work to maintain relationships. Water and corn starch are combined in a particular ratio, so that when you knead it, it's a pliable solid, but if you stop kneading, it immediately liquefies and runs through your fingers.

"Please follow the recipe," said Dea. "One time, I forgot to bring the recipe with me, and I told the people who were assisting me to just wing it. They didn't know the right ratio, and it turned into soup.

"You'll need to move through the crowd, handing them the oogley and letting them hand it back to you. Please use the bowl – I suspect a lot of these pastors will be wearing their Sunday clothes, and so the less corn starch we can get on them the better. We're going to get some corn starch on them – that's just the nature of the beast – but let's try not to make a bigger mess than we have to.

"Schuyler, can you go behind them with a wet towel to let the people wipe their hands after they handle the oogley?"

All of the team would participate in some role-playing skits at various points in the day.

"Where are the pastors going to stay?" asked Axel.

"Well, a lot of them are going to take an overnight bus tonight, be here for the seminar tomorrow, and then take an overnight bus home so that they can be back at their normal churches for service on Sunday."

"Ouch," said Axel.

"The pastors are eager for this kind of training," said Pastor Joe. "There is nothing exactly like it in Kenya."

"We will need to be here early to help set up in the morning," said Dea. "We won't have a team meeting *per se*, but we will have a devotion at 6:30 in the morning, and then get right to work. So everyone will need to adjust their morning schedules accordingly.

"All of you are invited to share our devotion with us tomorrow, by the way."

Jeff was scheduled for the Saturday devotional, but he hadn't planned on guests. He immediately began running through the message in his mind to see if it was cross-cultural, or if there was anything that might offend Kenyans in the group.

◆

The devotion was attended by all of the Americans and about six or eight Kenyans. After reviewing his notes Friday night, Jeff decided that only a few minor tweaks, and some added words of explanation, were needed to make it cross-cultural.

The devotion had to do with cast-iron cookware and how Jeff had gotten to tour a factory that made it while attending the National Cornbread Festival in South Pittsburg, Tenn. Jeff talked about how things like cars become less valuable the more they are used, while cast iron cookware becomes more valuable, because it builds up a patina called "seasoning." He tied that into a verse from James about the testing of our faith producing endurance.

"You are a fine speaker, Jeff," said Pastor Joe afterward. "Perhaps God is calling you to become a pastor."

"I have not heard that call."

"Perhaps you should listen more closely."

Even before the devotion had ended, a few pastors had made their way to the church, taking matatus from the bus station downtown. As soon as the devotional broke, the team began setting up the registration table.

The team was introduced briefly once the conference was underway, but once it started individual team members could sit in or wander out into the courtyard, staying nearby so that they could be summoned quickly when it was time for a skit or other activity. The team tried to make sure at least one member was in the sanctuary at any given time to keep track of what was coming up.

The workshop was a mix of Biblical principles and general leadership and management training. It started out with common myths about leadership, the qualities of an effective leader, and so on. Many of the pastors serving small churches in remote rural locations had little or no training and were eager for the information.

Jeff, at mid-morning, was seated in the courtyard, hunched over, hands on his knees. Schuyler came over and sat down next to him.

"How do you feel?" she said. "Is something wrong?"

"No, I'm fine. I'm just ... tired. I've been running on adrenaline for a week and a half, and today is sort of anti-climactic, and I'm not making soap, and I have the chance to sit here in the courtyard and it's all catching up to me. I'm tired. I want to go home to Tennessee and have a cheeseburger and tots."

"Why did you have to go and mention a cheeseburger and tots? Now you've got *me* hungry."

It was almost tea time. The ladies of the church were preparing the tea, but Dea had insisted that the team help serve it, Americans working alongside the Kenyans.

The Kenyan church ladies agreed but still seemed a little suspicious about the idea, as if their hospitality was somehow being called into question.

In a similar demonstration of equality, Dea's first action on arriving at the church Saturday morning had been to personally rip down the sign from the Mzungu outhouse and stash the padlock in her tote bag. She told Jeff later that she felt certain the church would have done something similar anyway – after all, today almost everyone in the sanctuary was an honored guest, so it was impractical to limit the guests to one stall or the other – but she didn't want to take any chances, and she didn't want any of the visiting pastors to know what the situation had been during the week.

At lunch, the church ladies would do the serving themselves but the team was directed to scatter among the visiting pastors and join them for the meal.

Fortunately, the meal for the day was lentils, which Jeff found somewhat less disgusting than sukuma wiki. He chatted with two pastors from the Kisii region – one tall, dignified and quiet, the other enthusiastic and outgoing. Both asked about the chances of Salt+Water sending a team to their church to do cottage industry training.

"Teddy and Dea make those decisions," said Jeff. "I don't have a thing to do with it."

Jeff looked around at lunch and didn't see Lucy anywhere. She'd been in the office earlier, working on the certificates. He excused himself from the visiting pastors and went to the office. Sure enough, Lucy was sitting there, still working on the certificates.

"There's no Coke in the fridge today," she told Jeff. "I've checked already.

"You eating lunch?" he asked.

"I hate to admit this – I fell asleep at the desk this morning. I woke up from the sound of everyone in the courtyard, but I figured I needed to get these done."

"You've got time to get them done. We're all

tired; we're all running on fumes. You need to eat something. You look awful."

"Funny, coming from you. How many lunches have you eaten this week?"

Jeff turned beet red. "Who else besides you knows I haven't been eating lunch?"

"Everyone. Including Teddy and Dea. I think even Joe and Helen know."

Jeff winced.

"Well, look at me -- I could stand to miss a few meals. And I've eaten like a pig at the house in the evenings. You need to eat something."

"Don't say things like that about yourself," said Lucy.

"You need to eat something."

"Don't change the subject."

"That *was* the subject."

"I will go get lunch -- if you will promise me not to say another word for the rest of the trip about your weight, or what you wish you had done in the soapmaking workshop, or the young man who got splashed in the eye."

"I don't mean it. That's what a jerk I am – I'm just fishing for affirmation, and the quickest way to get it is to badmouth myself. That's how selfish I am."

"You obviously do mean it, whether you realize it or not – or why else would you need the affirmation so badly?"

"I ... uh ...."

"My deal stands. I will go get lunch, and you don't say another word bad about yourself for the rest of the trip. I want you to promise."

"I promise."

"I am deadly serious about this, Jeff Doerman. I will be listening."

◆

The oogley demonstration came soon after lunch, which meant some scrambling – the bowl that Dea had planned for Jeff and Kate to use for mixing the oogley had been picked up with the dirty dishes after lunch, and Axel had to go find the kitchen ladies and get it back.

Jeff hoped the kitchen ladies hadn't already appropriated his soapmaking pots and bowl.

Oogley was a great success – it worked perfectly, and the pastors were delighted with the seemingly-magic properties of the corn starch mixture.

The rest of the day went off smoothly. Lucy got the certificates done soon after lunch and was able to relax for the rest of the afternoon.

The certificates were awarded at the end of the day, and the pastors hailed matatus to go back downtown to the bus station.

"Imagine how tired they'll be by the time they get home," said Teddy."

"Don't have to," said Schuyler.

Teddy gathered the team together for a brief huddle.

"Thanks to all of you for your hard work today. We'll leave for the safari park at 5:30 in the morning." There were a few groans, but he continued.

"We will be riding on a safari van to Masai Mara. It will be about an eight-hour drive. We will need some cooperation. I don't think we will have room on the van for all of our luggage. I need you tonight to put what you will need for the safari park into one suitcase. The other suitcases will be locked up at Joe and Helen's house, and we will pick them up when we get back to Nairobi for our flight out on Tuesday."

There were some rolled eyes over this announcement, but no objections were spoken out loud. There was, however, a question.

"We're taking an eight-hour van ride tomorrow," said Lucy. "Can we wear pants?"

"We told you at training that you could wear pants or shorts at debrief," said Dea. "The dress thing was just while we were at our work site, because we didn't know the customs or the sensibilities of the people at the church."

"Right. But will it offend our host families or anyone if that's how we get dressed tomorrow morning? If we're traveling cross-country, I'd rather be comfortable. Plus, if I can't pack everything, I want to pack comfortably."

"Absolutely. We won't be at the church at all tomorrow, and I don't think any of our host families would be shocked or offended. But thanks for asking, and thanks to all three of you for your cooperation on this."

"And you too, darling," said Teddy. "We will stop by Joe and Helen's house when we return to Nairobi on Tuesday, and so there will be a chance to shower or change clothes or transfer things back and forth between your two cases before we head to the airport Tuesday night."

"Don't forget to have some closure tonight with your families," said Dea. "You should have brought some sort of small, symbolic gift for your hosts, and tonight is the time to give it to them."

## ELEVEN
### Crossing the Great Rift

The family gifts, Teddy and Dea had said during training, were supposed to be inexpensive; they were symbolic, and not something large enough to create jealousy. It was suggested, though not required, that they be representative of the giver's region or home state.

Jeff's gift for the family, which he'd brought with him from Tennessee, was a wooden box of pencils, with a sliding cover. Axel had brought a selection of jellies from a specialty food business in his county. George and Elizabeth appeared delighted with both, but there was no way to know if they were just being polite.

There was no doubt about Sally's reaction when Axel gave her the Jenga game.

"I hope we have not been an inconvenience," said Jeff. "We really appreciate your hospitality."

"You have been no inconvenience at all," said George. "It has been our honor, and our pleasure."

It had been a long day, and everyone was eager to get to bed early. It would be a very, very early morning.

George drove Jeff, Axel and their luggage to Pastor Joe's house first thing in the morning. Joe and Helen's house was not far at all from George and Elizabeth's, and was in the same type of fenced-in development.

The unused bags were stashed in what had been Lucy, Kate and Schuyler's bedroom for the past week, and the traveling luggage was wedged into the van and on top. Jeff noted there was an odd little cap covering most of the roof of the van.

"Anyone who needs to use the facilities," said Teddy, "should do so now."

After several team members took Teddy's advice, the team circled up.

"You will not attend worship this Sunday," said Pastor Joe, "but I hope this will be the beginning of a restful Sabbath for you. You have honored God with all you have done this week. I would like to pray for your safe travel, and that you will enjoy yourself at Masai Mara."

And so, after a prayer by Joe for traveling mercies, the Salt+Water Ministries Kenya team boarded the van and hit the road. It was 5:45 a.m.

"Why don't you take shotgun, Jeff?" suggested Teddy.

Shotgun could be both a blessing and a curse, Jeff knew. In a situation like this, with so much new to see, it was exciting to sit up front. But in a van, it also tended to isolate him from what was going on in the back. He also suspected that the suggestion was related to his size, and he didn't necessarily like to be reminded of being overweight.

The driver, Simon, would answer questions but obviously wasn't interested in a conversation.

They headed north on what seemed to be a main highway. There were scruffy-looking buildings facing the highway – all with painted logos of Mortein Doom, Colgate toothpaste, Eveready batteries and a host of Kenyan products, or at least products with which Jeff was not familiar. There were pedestrian bridges crossing over the highway close to town; then, as the van got away from Nairobi, they disappeared. They turned off onto a two-lane highway and began heading west. There were occasional gas stations or little towns – each with its little Coca-Cola kiosk and a place that sold Celtel or Safaricom cell phone minutes.

They wound up into the hills. Jeff tried to journal, but the highway was just too rough. In cases, the pavement had crumbled away to nothing or was being repaired, and the van would have to veer off into rutted clay on either side of the road.

There were also checkpoints from time to time. Tire spikes blocked half of the road, so you had to slow down and weave around them while officers of some sort – police? Military? Did the distinction even matter? - watched you pass. None of the checkpoints ever stopped the van, so Jeff figured that weary American tourists didn't fit whatever profile they were looking for.

"We seem to be pretty high up," said Axel.

The team tried to get a view through the thinning trees to the left of the highway, but couldn't see much. Then, up ahead, there was a parking lot to the left. The van pulled in and to a stop.

There was a souvenir shop.

There was a big rock.

There was a rusted, weather-beaten sign with a Coca-Cola logo. The wording on the sign appeared to have been painted and repainted several times. The current wording read "WELCOME TO THE GREAT RIFT VALLEY VIEW POINT – ALT 2140 METRES." That was, Jeff figured, more than 7,000 feet – 1,500 feet higher than Nairobi, 1,700 feet higher than Denver.

The shop, the big rock and the sign were all secondary.

What there mostly was, was the view.

"It's like God looking down on creation," said Teddy, his jaw dropping.

The view from the bluff into the Great Rift Valley was, indeed, breathtaking. You could see fields and roads, and – strangely enough – a little island of gigantic satellite dishes, or something that looked like gigantic satellite dishes. (Jeff imagined the secret underground lair of a James Bond villain.) There were hills in the distance, but they were so far away they hardly seemed noticeable. It seemed as if you should almost be able to pick up on the curve of the earth.

Several people tried taking photos, but it was impossible to convey the sheer scale with the normal photo lens. It just looked like a photo taken out of the window of an airplane.

Eventually, the team members tore themselves away from the view and wandered into the souvenir shop. It was nice to look at Maasai market-style souvenirs without anyone following them around.

Jeff bought two bottles of Stoney Tangawizi and offered the second one to Axel, who didn't care for it and ended up handing it off to Kate. Jeff also bought a bottled water to save for later.

There were rudimentary plumbing facilities at the souvenir stand -- they were none too clean or well-maintained, and the group had to once again use their vanishing supplies of toilet paper.

Eventually, of course, it was time to get back onto the road.

The road continued to hug the bluff for another few miles, then started to wind its way down.

Simon, the driver, spoke up as the road reached the bottom to point out a beautiful little stone chapel by the roadside.

"That was built by Italian prisoners during World War II," he said. "They helped to build this road, and they were treated well by the British, and they built this chapel."

Jeff turned around and repeated the story to Teddy and Schuyler in the second row. Teddy and Dea had been sitting together before the Great Rift Valley stop, but apparently they decided they no longer needed intense consultation with each other on upcoming projects.

Schuyler passed the story along to the rest of the rear cabin.

The road through the valley passed not far from the huge satellite dishes. Were they radio telescopes? Some sort of orbital tracking station for NASA? Simon had no idea.

*No, Mr. Bond ... I expect you to die ....*

It was not long before the van reached the city of Narok, larger than, but just as dusty and tattered as, the little roadside towns. On the far side of Narok was a service station which had a convenience store with a little snack bar. Jeff bought some samosas, some potato chips, a Cadbury chocolate bar for dessert and some chewing gum for later. He passed on the

Tangawizi and went for good old reliable Coca-Cola.

The snack bar had pay toilets – the user had to pay an attendant, who handed him or her a small wad of toilet paper on the way in.

As some of the group members stood around the van, waiting for the rest to show up, Teddy put his hand on Jeff's shoulder.

"You know, pal, you did a fine job in church the other day. Would you be interested in maybe preaching one service on the next trip?"

There was no question in Teddy's mind, apparently, that there would be a next trip. There was little question in Jeff's.

"I might."

"I think God may be using you in ways you don't understand yet."

Just then, a Kenyan approached them.

"Are you pastors?" he asked, apparently having heard a little of the conversation.

"I am not ordained," said Teddy, "although I sometimes preach."

"Do you have a Bible?"

"I have a Bible," said Jeff. He darted onto the van, grabbed his backpack, and pulled out the modest little hardback New International Version which he'd brought on the trip.

"Here," he said, handing it to the man.

"Thank you." He shook Jeff's and Teddy's hands.

As the van left Narok, Jeff looked out the

passenger side window and saw the man sitting on a bench in front of the store, reading his Bible.

"I have five different Bibles on my shelf back home," said Jeff. "Different translations, study Bibles, different sizes. I feel like a miser, or a spendthrift, or ... something."

"I have seven," said Teddy.

"We don't realize how much we have back home, do we?"

As they got back onto the highway, Jeff started noticing more and more other vehicles – vans and SUVs -- with various Safari-related logos.

Lucy, however, noticed something else.

"Zebras!" she squealed, loudly enough to be heard throughout the van. Sure enough, in the open African countryside, a ways off from the road, were about eight or ten zebras.

Jeff knew, or assumed, that they would be seeing plenty of wildlife at Masai Mara, but there was something magic about seeing an exotic animal running free in the populated countryside.

And the zebras were not the last such find, either. A few miles down the road, Axel caught a glimpse of a baboon at the roadside.

The human landscape was changing as well. There were donkeys and other livestock in some of the little towns through which they passed. One donkey pulled a cart with two big blue plastic barrels like the ones Axel had used for water purification.

Simon said that some of the people on the roadside were Maasai, although at first they appeared in modern dress. But eventually, Dea saw a group of Maasai women wearing the tribe's iconic red wrap.

Jeff wondered what Kenya was like before the British got here, much less before Coca-Cola did.

He flipped through a little Kenya guidebook he had purchased at the souvenir shop on the rift escarpement, then turned around and asked Teddy why "Maasai," the name of the people, is spelled differently from "Masai Mara," the name of the wildlife refuge.

"It's the same name. Maasai is now considered a better phonetic spelling, and so it's used to respect their pronunciation. But it used to be spelled without that other 'a,' and it was back then that the name of the park was chosen."

"Giraffes!" squealed Lucy, so loudly that even Simon was startled.

Sure enough, there they were, off in the distance.

"You will see them much more closely on safari," said Simon.

Not long after that, the van turned off the highway onto a gravel-and-dirt road.

"We must be close," Schuyler said.

Schuyler was wrong.

The last leg of the trip took 90 dusty, bone-jarring minutes, but seemed much, much longer, over badly rutted roads. At several points, Simon pointed out little circular enclosures, made of sticks, that had mud huts arranged in a circle inside them.

"That is a Maasai village," said Simon.

Finally, eventually, the van pulled up to the entrance of the Karibu Mara Safari Lodge. As soon as the van pulled up, employees rushed to the van to welcome each member of the group with steamy hot towels and cool glasses of some sort of fruit juice.

"I like the looks of this," said Axel.

The group filed into the lobby. As Teddy and Dea spoke with the desk clerk, the rest of the group kept walking – on the far side of the lobby was a deck; it was part of what seemed to be a large restaurant or dining hall. From the expansive, open deck, you could see the oxbow bend of a river, just a few hundred yards away.

"What is the plural of 'hippopotamus'?", Jeff asked.

"Apparently," answered Schuyler, "*that* is."

Lounging in the river were at least a dozen hippos.

Teddy and Dea came to get the group and were startled to see the hippos. They were distracted themselves for a few seconds, but then refocused.

"If we hurry up and take our things to our rooms," said Teddy, we have time to go on a safari ride right away, and still be back by dinner. I know that may sound like the last thing you want to do after sitting in the van for eight hours, but we'll only have four chances while we're here, and this is one of them.

"It's completely up to you. Anyone who wants to go can go, and anyone who wants to stay can stay."

Schuyler and Dea said they wanted to stick around the safari park; Jeff, Lucy, Kate and Axel, plus Teddy himself, decided to go.

The team members each had to sign a room registration form, and keys were handed out.

The resort was laid out with a series of long cabins facing the river, each one made up of six or eight rooms, all with outside doors like a motel. Bellhops carried their luggage, and the team was in three adjoining rooms in one of the cabins. A cot had been arranged for the room that Lucy, Kate and Schuyler would share.

The rooms were comparable to any western hotel room, except for having no TV sets. Jeff tried out the bed and it felt wonderful.

"Second thoughts about the safari, buddy?" asked Axel.

"No. This is a once-in-a-lifetime thing. Plus, it's obviously a big deal to Lucy. Did you hear how she reacted when she saw that giraffe? I want to be there when she sees an elephant, or a lion."

Axel grinned.

"There you go, buddy. We've been at the safari park 15 minutes, and you're already turning into a wild animal."

◆

The van looked different when the group gathered in the lobby. The white "cap" on top had been pushed about a foot in the air on a metal framework, so that the passengers behind the front seat could stand up in the center aisle and see in all directions.

"I hate that Dea and Schuyler are going to miss this, but I'm glad I don't have to take shotgun," said Jeff.

"I bet you are," said Lucy.

"Dea saw something on the bulletin board about massage," said Teddy. "They have a masseuse here. They had an opening, and I think she should be getting started right about now. Schuyler is going to go tomorrow.

"It costs extra, by the way – and obviously, you're responsible for something like that -- but the price looked to be quite reasonable, if anyone else wants to take advantage tomorrow some time."

Jeff had paid little attention to Kate's digital SLR during the work week, but he noted now that she had apparently brought a long zoom lens along on the trip, and it was now on the camera.

"You should get some great shots," said Jeff, whose little digital point-and-shoot didn't have anything but useless "digital zoom."

Of course, he wondered how Kate could afford a nice camera, but then he remembered that her family ran an office supply store, and if that meant computers it might also mean access to digital cameras.

They boarded the van and sat in their seats until they were sure what the plan was.

The van pulled out of the resort compound and turned right, into the savannah, tall grass interrupted by occasional trees or bushes and cris-crossed by dirt and gravel roads.

Simon got on what looked like a CB radio and spoke in Swahili to someone on the other end, who responded in kind.

They drove on for a while, and at the first sight of wildlife – tiny, deer-like creatures which Simon said were called dik-dik – everyone stood up in the aisle and began looking out. At first, there were several false alarms -- "Is that something? Over there?" -- to the point that Simon was noticeably amused.

But then, a mile or two from the resort, they saw the elephants.

Simon conversed quickly on his CB, and then – looking around as if he were about to do something untoward – he drove the van off the gravel road through the field so that his passengers could get a closer look.

These were not circus elephants, or even zoo elephants. They were gathered around a small stand of trees, munching on leaves. One had a broken tusk and looked about 50,000 years old. But all of them had a stateliness to them. They paid no more mind to the safari van than Jeff would have paid to an ant crawling by. They were not the prisoners, or even the guests, of humanity. Humanity hardly figured into their planning at all.

"What a sight," whispered Lucy.

Jeff could have watched the elephants forever, but eventually Simon indicated that it might be best to move on. He got back onto the beaten path and continued his route.

The radio crackled to life. After a brief conversation, Simon turned the van around and started heading back the other way.

"What's going on?" asked Teddy.

"Lions," said Simon.

"I hope we're heading toward them, and not away from them," Jeff said to Axel.

They were, in fact, heading towards the lions – but too late. The van came upon a cluster of other safari vans, with tourists peering off into the distance, but the lions had apparently disappeared into the high grass a hundred yards away. Still, the people in the vans kept staring, in hopes the lions would emerge. That didn't seem to be happening, and after 10 minutes or so of waiting, Simon advised moving on.

"I want to see lions," said Lucy, despairingly.

"You will see them," said Simon. "Maybe tomorrow."

Over a little rise, the van encountered another safari van moving in the opposite direction. The two vans stopped and the drivers chatted briefly. Simon laughed at something the other driver said, and waved at the other driver as he continued on his way. Simon contiued.

"Watch to your right up here," he said.

There were giraffes. Simon turned right down a dirt road to get closer to them, and he ended up close enough that Kate didn't really need her zoom lens and even Jeff was able to get a wonderfully-detailed photo. They moved with remarkable awkward grace.

A few miles down the road, there were what Axel called water buffalo – but water buffalo are Asian, not African, and Simon said these were cape buffalo.

"You will see many of them," he said. "The migration is passing through this area now."

They saw jackals, and vultures, and zebras, and gazelles. Soon, though, it was clear that the sun was on its way down, and Adam began heading back in the direction of the safari lodge.

The sunset was beautiful, and the four of them with cameras took photos of it. Kate kept trying to get the perfect composition, and Jeff finally had to reach out his hand and put it over her lens.

"Look at it," said Jeff. "Just look at it."

It was a hard balance to draw; on the one hand, this was a once-in-a-lifetime opportunity, and Kate, like Jeff, wanted to preserve it for the future. Jeff wanted to be able to put together a slide show for the partners who had given so generously to send him to Africa.

But there comes a point, Jeff knew, when the traveler spends so much time looking through a viewfinder, or at an LCD screen, that he or she starts to miss the details of what is happening around him.

Kate looked at Jeff quizzically, then put the camera down and looked at the sunset.

A few seconds later, a tear rolled down her cheek.

## TWELVE
### Bruce Cockburn Can Stop Wondering

Dea and Schuyler were sitting on the deck, near the bar, sipping on bottled waters when the rest of the team came back.

"Habari za safari?" asked Dea.

"Words can't do it justice," said Teddy. We saw elephants, and giraffes, and ... words can't do it justice. I can't wait for you to see it tomorrow. How was the massage?"

Dea just wiggled her shoulders and smiled.

Team Safari returned to their rooms to freshen up for supper and then returned to the lobby and the open-air dining room.

The meals at Karibu Mara were served buffet

style. A few things on the menu seemed vaguely European, but Schuyler said many of the other guests at the resort were Europeans, with a small scattering of Americans thrown in. In any case, the food was wonderful, and much closer to American food than anything they'd eaten in Kenya, except maybe the grilled meats at Carnivore.

There was, at one station, sukuma wiki and ugali, perhaps a nod to Kenyan cuisine for tourists who fancied themselves culturally curious.

Jeff decided to pass on that part of the menu.

The cost of the food was included in the room rate, Dea advised the group, but soft drinks, wine or bottled water were extra, billed to the diner's hotel room.

"Any additional expenses are billed to your room," she said, "including the gift shop, and the masseuse, and what have you. So you and your roommate need to make sure you keep track of your individual expenses. You can settle up at the front desk when we check out."

Axel blessed the meal and all seven of them tore into the food eagerly, distracted from time to time by the movement of the hippos in the bend of the river nearby. Lucy and Kate were in furious conversation about the animals they had seen, and Jeff could hardly get a word in edgewise. He turned to Schuyler.

"We know that Dea got a massage," said Jeff.

"What did you do while we were gone?"

"The pool is open, but it's a little too cool to be any fun right now," she said. "So I laid out on a deck chair and got some sun."

Dusk finally faded into night, and while Jeff could still tell the hippos were out there, he couldn't see them well enough to sit and stare.

"Our original plan was to start debrief tonight," said Teddy, as the meal was winding down. "But it's been a long day, and I don't think any of us would be paying full attention.

"In the morning, we will have a safari drive at 7 a.m. -- completely optional, but highly recommended – and then breakfast will be served after that. Then we'll do some debrief tomorrow morning, eat lunch, and a little bit more debrief right after lunch.

"Late tomorrow afternoon, we will have another safari drive. Then dinner, then a little more debrief, and we will close the evening with communion tomorrow night.

"Tuesday morning, we will check out early and have a short safari drive on our way out of the park. We'll try to pack some sort of take-along breakfast, that day, if we can talk the kitchen here into selling us something.

"Enjoy the rest of your evening, and sleep well tonight."

◆

After dinner, Jeff and Axel adjourned to their

room. Axel stretched out on top of the covers -- "just to rest my eyes for a minute" -- and was out like a light seconds later.

Jeff pulled his journal out of his bag and started to write.

Axel, at that point, started to snore.

Jeff closed the journal, grabbed the room key, and headed back towards the lobby. He ordered a Coke from the bar. They didn't have Tangawizi; the normal clientèle of Europeans and Americans probably didn't order it much.

He sat at a table and listened to the gentle splashing noises from the hippos nearby.

A tall man in his 60s, wearing a golf shirt and carrying a mineral water, came over.

"You American?" he asked, in the kind of flat Midwestern non-accent favored by TV newscasters.

"I am."

"You been here long?"

"We got here this afternoon. We've been on one drive." Jeff waved his hand, palm up, towards the chair next to him.

"I've been here three days," said the man, sitting down. "I took the hot air balloon safari this morning. Incredible."

"How much does that cost?"

"About $400. It was worth it."

"Out of my price range, unfortunately. I'm just here for two nights on the tail end of a mission trip."

"Mission trip? Evangelizing the natives?"

"More relief work. Not so much evangelism."

"As far as your relief work goes, I wish you luck, but I'm not sure Africa can be saved," he said. "My company has tried to break into this market from time to time. The corruption's incredible.

"The first time I ever came here, I saw a banner on one of the government buildings: 'This is a corruption-free zone.' I swear. How bad, how open does the corruption have to be before they actually have to *hang banners* outside the building claiming they're not corrupt? They're never going to be able to solve their problems and grow until they can get the government cleaned up – and I doubt they can ever get the government cleaned up. And until then, anything we try to do is going to be useless. I don't mean to be rude, but I think you just wasted a week if you were trying to help Kenyans."

"I wasn't trying to save the whole country. I was trying to help a few people."

"Same difference. When you get back to the States, they're all going to e-mail you asking you to send them $500. If they can't or won't solve their own problems, why should we?"

"Well, we probably caused some of the problems."

"Sure. Blame the bad old West. We've tried to bring business, and progress, and modern medicine. We were clumsy sometimes, or naive, or what have you, but you can't say that Africa is our fault."

"You can't?"

"Politicians or academics blame us. Not real people. Not people who've been here."

"When you've been here," Jeff asked, "have you been to the Kibera slums?"

"No. They tell me it's not very safe."

"I thought so. I, uh, probably need to get back to my journal." Jeff picked up his book and started writing as the man walked off in search of more compatible company.

Jeff journaled about Africa.

*I don't know whose fault this is,* wrote Jeff. *But it's not the fault of the people I'm working with. And even if it were, I'm not sure that would get me off the hook.*

He realized someone was walking up behind him, and looked up just in time to see Lucy take the seat where the Ugly American had been just a few minutes before.

"Hi," she said.

"Hello. I'm surprised to see you."

"Why?"

"I figured you and Kate would be playing Scrabble, or braiding each other's hair, or talking about your favorite boy bands."

"You're very funny, you know that?"

"How did you like the safari drive today?"

"Words don't do it justice."

"I know," said Jeff, closing his journal. "I made

notes of what animals we saw, but that sounds like we went to the zoo."

"That was *not* a zoo."

"No. It was not. Teddy says most of the camps are located inside Masai Mara – inside the wildlife refuge – but this one isn't, which is why we were on a back road and why we didn't have to stop and pay to get in. But it is on a protected reserve, and it's under a lot of the same restrictions.

"The drivers aren't supposed to get off the roads, and they can be fined on the spot – but they also work for tips, and if they think  they can get their customers a closeup view, they'll take their chances."

"Will we have to tip the driver?"

"Teddy and Dea have that figured into the budget. Their travel agent gave them a lot of good information like that."

"I tell you, Jeff, staying at a place like this, I almost feel guilty. I think of all the people who gave money to send me here."

"Well, you at least paid some of your own way, or I assume you did. You can say that the part you paid was for the safari. I'm out of luck; I didn't pay any of my own way."

"Are you bad-mouthing yourself?"

"No. That was a statement of fact."

"It sounded like self-pity to me."

"Maybe a little."

"Remember our deal," she said.

"I'm back on the high road. Seriously, though – I expected you to be in the room with Kate. You two have been joined at the hip all week."

"We were outside trying to see if we could see anything, you know, in the river, and your windows were open. I heard one person snoring, but not two. I figured Axel was snoring, and I took a chance you were here."

"I'm glad you did. I wanted to see you."

"I wanted to see you, too. I've thought about you a lot this week."

"Really?"

"Why is that so hard for you to believe? Why wouldn't someone want to think about Jeff Doerman?"

"It's not me – it's you. I've tried talking to you in the past, Lucy. And you've always been very polite, and I can even say you've been a good friend, for the short time we've known each other. But you've always kept me entirely at arm's length. I'm a complete idiot at relationships, but even I can tell when I'm being kept at arm's length.

"I don't want to talk about me. I need for this not to be about me. I want to talk about you for a while."

Lucy thought about this, and the two of them were silent for a minute, listening to the splashing from the river below.

"You're right. As lonely as I am, I don't want to let people in. My pastor told me I have 'intimacy problems.' I hate that term.

"But I also have news for you. You're not the only one who feels awkward around the opposite sex or who feels like they missed out on ... the picket fence thing.

"I guess I have shut you out sometimes. I didn't want to lead you on, because you seemed ... needy, and I didn't think I was interested. But I've seen you this week in a way I never saw you before. I know you got frustrated with your workshop, but I saw you caring for those people, and throwing yourself into this trip. I saw you in a way you don't even see yourself.

"When we were at the Blixen museum the other day, we were talking about Denys Finch Hatton. I thought of Denys from the movie, you thought of Denys from the book.

"But as I sat there, looking out at the hills ...."

Just then, Schuyler walked into view.

"Lucy! Jeff! I'm glad to see somebody's still up. I was going stir-crazy in my cabin."

"Hello, Schuyler."

"Lucy ... where's Kate?"

"She's back in the room taking a long hot shower. I mean a long ... hot ... shower."

Schuyler turned to Jeff. "The hot water didn't really work well in our bathroom at Pastor Joe's house. They had this weird electric shower head, and it kept blowing the breaker."

"Axel says it's called a 'widowmaker.' Ours worked OK, though. Why didn't you say anything about this at team meetings?"

"It didn't seem that important," said Lucy, "and Joe and Helen worked so hard to make us feel at home every other way."

"Is there anything to do out here?" Schuyler asked.

"Not really. You can get soft drinks at the bar."

"I may get a glass of wine, if you two can keep your mouths shut."

"I know you meant that in fun," said Jeff, "but I would only take a drink if there were zero chance of Teddy seeing you. Zero chance."

"Teddy has seen people drink before. Just because he's recovering alcoholic doesn't mean he's never around people who drink."

"Well, still."

"Here," said Lucy. "Sit with us and have a Coke." She got up and went to the bar to get two Cokes, as Schuyler sat on the other side of Jeff.

She looked at Jeff for a few seconds.

"Is something wrong?"

"No, Schuyler."

"Something's wrong."

"Nothing's wrong."

"I interrupted something, didn't I?"

Jeff sensed a sadness in Schuyler's voice and thought of her and Rob sitting on their back porch back in Tennessee, laughing and grilling hamburgers and making room for their sad-sack fifth-wheel friend.

"Absolutely not. Lucy and I were just sitting here listening to the hippopotami."

Lucy and Jeff and Schuyler sat and talked for a while, about Africa, and the week at the church, and the souvenirs they would be taking home.

"You know," said Schuyler, "I have UNO cards."

"Let's go back to my room," said Lucy. "Kate's probably decent by now, but if her hair is wet, she may just not want to come out. She's probably wondering where I am anyway."

As they walked back to Lucy and Kate's room, Lucy whispered in Jeff's ear.

"I'll talk to you tomorrow," she said.

◆

Kate was still up, and decent, and the four of them gathered in Kate's room and played UNO for about an hour before Schuyler and Jeff finally excused themselves and went their separate ways to bed.

Axel had, at some point, awakened and changed out of his clothes; he was now asleep under the covers.

Jeff crawled into bed, absolutely exhausted but with his mind on overload. He finally lulled himself to sleep by thinking about the hippos a few hundred yards away, splashing and splashing with seemingly no care in the world.

Morning came soon enough, and this time the entire team gathered in front of the lodge to wait for the safari van. The van drivers apparently had their own parking and lodging in an area a few yards away from the resort.

When everyone was gathered and the van was present, it was time to load up. Jeff hesitated; today, there was a full cabin, and someone would have to take the front passenger seat. That person would have no way to stand up and take photos out of the roof.

"I'll take shotgun," said Teddy. "You had it yesterday."

Jeff felt guilty about this, but he accepted it.

They headed out in what seemed to be a different direction. The radio was all a-crackle, and Simon conversed happily with his fellow drivers.

The first wildlife they saw was a huge herd of the cape buffalo, far more than they had seen the previous day. Some were on one side of the road, some on the other.

There were a few more dik-dik, which Schuyler proclaimed "adorable," and some gazelles, their taller, skinnier cousins.

Everyone looked at Schuyler and Dea, who were suitably impressed.

Up ahead, there were three safari vans and an SUV parked, looking at something on the opposite side of a small rise. Simon pulled up beside them.

"Look over there," he said.

The grass was a little thinner here, and patchy, allowing a clear view of the lion as he passed by. He was traveling at an angle not quite perpendicular to the road, from the far left towards the somewhat closer right. He wasn't particularly close to the vans, but he wasn't trying to avoid them either. Like the elephants, he seemed completely unimpressed by the humans, as predators or prey.

Simon offered a pair of binoculars to Teddy, who looked and then passed them back to Jeff. Jeff marveled at the incredible muscle structure of the lion's forelegs, which seemed both taut and relaxed as the great beast strode forward.

"I keep thinking, 'I wish Rob could be here to see this,'" said Schuyler, softly.

They saw some more elephants – two this time, plus a baby – and enjoyed not only the experience itself but watching Dea and Schuyler for their reactions.

"I wish I had done this yesterday," said Dea.

"You were exhausted," said Teddy. "You wouldn't have enjoyed it."

The van returned to the lodge and it was time for breakfast. Jeff was thrilled to discover a made-to-order omelet bar was part of the buffet.

"Axel," he said, "care for some conflicts in the morning?"

"No," Axel responded, "I'm going for the waffles."

◆

"So," said Dea, "we've been to Africa. And we've seen poverty – for some of us, it's a kind of poverty we've never seen before. Then again, every poverty is different, so I guess for all of us it's a kind of poverty we've never seen before."

The team was seated in folding chairs in a circle on the lawn, on the opposite side of the lodge from most of the guest rooms. Jeff shifted in his chair and took a swig from his bottled water.

Dea continued. "A college professor named Kurt ver Beek published a study in 2005 criticizing short-term mission trips. His study found that such trips did little real, permanent good for the people where they were working, which a lot of people had already suspected, but he also found that the trips had little long-term effect on the short-term missionaries.

"Defenders of short-term missions – people like me -- sometimes portray it as something that helps open the eyes of Christians back home – changes our attitudes, makes us more willing to send money to worthy long-term mission projects, and what have you. But ver Beek's study didn't find those changes.

"Teddy and I founded this ministry because we wanted to do something different. We didn't want to parachute in, build a church, and then ride off into the sunset."

"If you parachute in and ride off," said Teddy, "you've apparently stolen a horse at some point. That can't be good for evangelism."

Dea rolled her eyes but otherwise ignored him. "Teddy and I promise you that we will continue to follow up with Joe and Helen and track how and if the cottage industry workshops are being put into play. It may be that we didn't give them quite enough to get a good start, and we may need to do advanced workshops next year. Or they may surprise us and start running right away. But I promise you we will stay in contact and we will report back to you on what is going on. We hope that, by planting seeds, we have made more of an impact than if we had built that second story that Pastor Joe wants so badly.

"But our more immediate question, here at debrief, is this – how were we affected by this trip? How will we be affected in the weeks to come?

"I've taken people to see this kind of poverty and had them swear to me – swear to me – that they would never go to a shopping mall again, never eat a fast food meal, never buy anything frivolous. None of those people ever stuck to that oath. I certainly couldn't.

"The question is, how *will* you be affected? What changes can you allow God to make in your life, and your attitude, and your heart, that will make this trip mean something? How will this trip affect your attitude towards illegal aliens, for example? Will you wonder what kind of conditions they left behind in their home country?

"Will you change your diet? Will you look a little harder for international news, especially about Kenya? Will you patronize certain companies, or avoid certain companies, because of how they treat this part of the world? Or is that too much to ask?

"You can't live your life in a vacuum. In order to make changes, you have to have the support of a community. Hopefully, we can support each other in living our lives a new way.

"Another part of this experience will be how you share your story back home. You all have friends, and family members, and financial partners who are anxious to hear from you – up to a point. But there comes a point where they aren't necessarily going to be interested in every little detail. There comes a point where they may think you're getting carried away with things. It was just a two-week trip, after all. Short-term.

"Sometimes, the hardest thing you have to do after a mission trip is give a five-minute report during a church service. Because *you can't tell it all in five minutes!* But five minutes may be all you get.

"We're going to talk a little bit about your stories, and about how to tell the people back home about them. Just as you gave your testimonies, and told the people of Kenya about your life back home, you have to tell the people back home about your trip to Kenya – and some of it just isn't going to translate.

"What I want us to do right now is go around the

circle and talk about one thing – one thing – we are taking home from Kenya. Axel?"

"I'm going to think about those boys at the orphanage. No one should have to live without parents in a little room next to a church – but they're loved, and they're taken care of, and they have a lot better attitude than I would if I were in their situation." He turned and looked at Kate.

"When the kids and their parents thought they had to give back their arts and craft projects, I though about, not only what we have in America, but what we expect in America – what we think we deserve, or would if we ever did think about it. What we take for granted."

"I think," said Jeff, "I think I will remember how much I pitied the people who lived in the Kibera slums, and then how proud Andrew was to have guests in his house, and I felt bad for having pitied him."

"I will remember the music," said Lucy. "That incredible music in church, and the joy and passion, and how close to Jesus I felt when I closed my eyes and got lost in that music."

"This isn't what you're looking for," said Schuyler, "but I will remember this team. I will remember the way we all focused on obeying God. Maybe we aren't doing what this professor thinks we ought to do, but we're trying to do something. And I will remember the way this team was so kind to me at a time when I really needed a little kindness – the way you gave me my space but stayed close enough to catch me."

Teddy smiled. "I think that's beautiful, Schuyler. It's not about what we were looking for; it's about what you need to say. That was perfect.

"As for me, I think I will remember Joe, and Helen, and how deeply they care about their people. Joe could very easily slip into being part of middle-class Nairobi and forget about the people of Kibera. But his passion is for helping those people, day in and day out, week in and week out."

Dea smiled. "I will remember seeing Axel's water purifier come to life, and seeing the eyes of the people in the church courtyard while they watched it bubble. I think of that Bible verse about giving a cup of cold water to one of God's children."

"This has been a good trip," said Teddy. "We have made some powerful memories. And those memories are important. At the same time, there is a danger – and I have to be constantly on guard against this – that this trip becomes about our experience, about the warm and fuzzy feelings, rather than about what we claim is our purpose for being here. We are part of this story, but this story is not about us."

## THIRTEEN
<u>Lucky for Jeff</u>

After lunch, Schuyler headed for her massage. Kate had snapped up the slot after that, and then Teddy.

Lucy and Jeff sat where they'd been the night before, looking out at the oxbow bend in the river and watching the hippos move around and refresh themselves in the warm midday sun.

"So," said Jeff, "before we were interrupted, I think you were talking about Mr. Denys Finch Hatton."

"He probably would have shot the lion this morning."

"And kept a stiff upper lip while doing it –

because he was *British.*"

"So he was. But when I was sitting there at the Blixen house, at the – what did you call it? -- the millstone table, looking back over the hills, I imagined myself living there, running a coffee plantation, trying to make a life, and I felt ... lonely. And Denys, no matter what accent he spoke in, would fly in and we'd be soul-mates and then he'd fly away and leave me to grow my coffee by myself."

"Honestly, Lucy, we weren't at the museum all that long."

"But then, I thought about what type of person I'd really like to be with if I were growing coffee on a plantation in the Ngong Hills. Not some guy in goggles and a leather helmet who flies away for months at a time, but ... someone I could be myself around. Someone who doesn't just stop over on his way to hunt big game."

He reached over and took her hand.

They sat there and watched the hippos for a few minutes, without saying a word.

Jeff stood up and offered her his hand to help her up. He put his arm around her waist and kissed her. He suspected he was lousy at it, and it wasn't a very long kiss.

"Thank you for believing in me," he said. "Thank you for letting me in."

"We're letting each other in. As needy as you think you are, you've been pretty good at keeping people out yourself."

"Lucy, I've been by myself for so long I might not be able to change. I'm past my freshness date. I'm so clueless about relationships I might be selfish, or stupid, or not know how to read the signals you're sending me. Maybe when we get back I'll turn into my old self again."

"I'm not exactly the goddess of love myself," she said. "What you're saying is that we might get hurt every now and then. Well, I guess that's right. Schuyler will tell you right now there are no guarantees. That's what we're talking about here: risk, which is part of what love is. And I think you're worth the risk. What was that quote about pride you read me from 'Out of Africa'?"

"Pride is faith in the idea that God had, when he made us." He stroked her cheek, then he grabbed her and kissed her again.

This time, he didn't stop to worry about his technique.

◆

Jeff and Lucy were standing in front of the lodge, holding hands, a few minutes before time for the afternoon safari drive. Teddy was the next to arrive.

"How was the massage?" Lucy asked.

"Terrific," he said. "I think my blood pressure dropped 20 points."

"Where's Dea?" asked Jeff.

"In the gift shop. Overpriced, and there's nothing

in there you couldn't get at the Great Rift Overlook for a lot less. But it's shopping." He looked at the two of them holding hands and raised an eyebrow.

"Are you holding on to him because you're afraid he's going to play in traffic?"

"That's it," said Lucy. "That's it exactly. I told him he had to hold my hand when we were near traffic."

Jeff was sure everyone else noticed, too, but no one else teased them about it -- until Axel took the passenger seat for the afternoon ride. He stepped up, but then thought about it and turned to Jeff

"Are you sure you don't want up here again, buddy?" Axel asked.

"No, Axel, I think you deserve the privilege."

"Because, I'm willing to sit all the way in the back row, with – what was your name again?"

"Karen Blixen."

" -- with Karen back there, and you can sit up here in front and watch the gazelles."

"Get in the van."

Axel saluted. "Yes, sir."

At the very end of the afternoon safari ride, as the light was beginning to fade, Simon was passing through an open area when Schuyler asked him to stop.

"I thought I saw something over there on the left."

Simon laughed, but he stopped. Teddy, Jeff and Kate, all of whom assumed the ride was winding down and had grown tired of standing awkwardly in the aisle, stood back up as the van stopped.

Moving through the tall grass were six dark forms. They passed into an open patch and revealed themselves: a pride of female lions.

"Wow," said Jeff.

"The light is terrible," said Kate, putting the camera to her eye, "but I'll try."

Jeff didn't feel as if he needed a photo to save the memory. He squeezed Lucy's hand, glanced at her and then looked back at the lions moving across the sunset.

◆

After dinner, there was a short debrief session, and then the group took a break as Teddy and Dea set up for communion. There was a small meeting room which the resort had allowed the group to use on short notice.

When the group re-convened, Teddy and Dea had a small, round loaf of bread and a goblet of ... something. It wasn't wine, at least not red wine, and it wasn't grape juice.

"We didn't even think about bringing grape juice from Nairobi," said Teddy, "and the resort doesn't have any. We thought about using wine from the bar, but we didn't want to offend anyone. This is ... passionfruit juice. It's not traditional, but I think it's strangely appropriate – since this is, after all, a symbol of Christ's passion, death and resurrection.

We know God will bless this bread and this juice to represent the body and blood of Christ."

Teddy read the Biblical account of the last supper. He held the loaf of bread and Dea held the goblet, and the congregants came forward one by one.

"The body of Christ, broken for you," said Teddy, as Jeff pinched off a piece of bread.

"The blood of Christ, shed for you," said Dea, as Jeff dipped the bread into the juice.

Jeff swallowed the morsel and dropped to his knees facing a wall.

*Dear Lord,* he prayed, *you have blessed me all my life, beyond all comprehension, and I have ignored it, denied it, discounted it, whined about it.*

*Forgive me, and give me a grateful heart and eyes to see the beauty of your creation, and the needs of those around me.*

*And thank you, Lord, for Lucy.*

◆

After the service, the team members had lingered a while in the meeting room, laughing and reminiscing. As people began to head their separate ways, Lucy and Jeff sat together at their place in the lodge and talked for two longer.

"Sometimes," Lucy said, "I get down on myself because I didn't get married right out of college like so many of my friends did. It feels like I've wasted the chance to share my life with somebody."

"I've felt that too."

"But if I had done that, I wouldn't be here with you right now."

Jeff wanted to sit there with Lucy all night, but they both knew that they had a long and tiring day of travel ahead of them and reluctantly parted company. Jeff tiptoed into the darkened room so he wouldn't wake up Axel.

"I thought your mother and I told you to be home by midnight," Axel mumbled.

"I'm sorry I woke you up," said Jeff. "I was trying to be quiet."

"I haven't been in bed that long. And there's a lot to think about. I've just been lying here.

"How'd it go with Lucy?"

"I should say that I feel like I'm 17 again, except that I was a pretty lonely 17-year-old. I guess I feel like I'm 17 for the first time. I just hope this isn't all going to go away when we get back to the States."

"Jeff, buddy, you think too much."

"People keep telling me that."

"It's too early to say something like this. It's way too early to say something like this. But I think you and Lucy are going to be great together."

◆

Teddy and Dea had bought some rolls, pastries and fresh fruit from the kitchen so that the team could eat breakfast in the van while on their way out of the area. Simon would take them on a 45-minute wildlife drive, working his way towards the road, and they would just head straight for Nairobi from there.

The team checked out and settled up their individual room accounts, then loaded up into the van and headed out.

The highlight of their last drive was giraffes. They saw what must have been a dozen giraffes at a stand of trees, and Simon got off the road in order to get them a closer look.

Soon, though, and with little fanfare, they were headed on their way out of the reserve. Because of their wildlife detour, they were taking a longer way back out to the highway than the one they had taken two days earlier, but the road was actually a little bit better, and so it didn't seem quite as long. They saw several more of the circular Maasai villages.

At one point, Simon pulled the van over at an abandoned building and everyone got out so that he could lower the expandable roof into its normal highway position.

"There would be too much wind once we get out onto the main road," he explained.

Jeff looked at the dingy, faded building, which was painted with a Mortein Doom logo.

"You know," he said to Lucy, "it's like we've been in Magical Giraffe Land for two days, and now it's back to the real Africa."

"I know. But this is the Africa we came here for."

"It is."

They got back onto the main highway and

headed for Narok.

In Narok, they stopped for gas and lunch. Axel, when Teddy and Dea weren't looking wandered out to the edge of the road, where various produce was being sold. He bought some roast corn and a stalk of sugar cane.

When the team sat down at a picnic table to eat what they'd bought at the gas station, Teddy noticed Axel's corn and cane.

"Where'd you get that?" he asked.

"Out by the road," said Axel.

"Have you eaten any of it?"

"I've had some of the corn. It's not very good. I was expecting the roast ears of corn like they have at the fair. But this is tough – it's like eating the unpopped popcorn from the bottom of the bowl."

Axel noted Teddy's annoyed expression.

"Why – what's wrong?"

"Probably nothing. I *hope* nothing. But Joe told me that there was a scam going a few months back where they sold drugged corn to people on the public cross-country buses, and then someone else would be waiting at the next stop to rob the person they'd drugged."

"Oh."

Teddy was starting to show his annoyance. "This is not a game, Axel. And the trip isn't over yet. We're trying to get all of you home safe."

"Hey, I'm *sorry*."

"Look," said Dea, "let's calm down a little. This is the part of the trip when people sometimes let their guards down. We have been an incredible team for almost two weeks now; let's see if we can make it home without any incidents."

"I'm sorry," said Teddy. "I should have said something in advance about dealing with the street vendors."

"I'm sorry too," said Axel.

"And I don't want you to go home thinking that Kenya is that kind of place. I mean, there are crime and criminals everywhere. I just want you to be careful."

"What's that other thing?" asked Kate.

"That's sugar cane," said Axel. "Someone told me about it at the church. They chew on this to clean their teeth."

"They chew on sugar cane ... to clean their teeth?" she asked.

"It's not as bad as it sounds," said Teddy. "It's not refined sugar, and the stringy texture does help clean their teeth."

"Is this safe to try?" asked Axel.

"After we get through eating, we can wash it off with some of the bottled water and peel it a bit," said Teddy. "Do you have your pocket knife with you?"

"I do," said Axel. "I've got to remember to pack it when we get to Pastor Joe's, so I don't have it on me at the airport."

After the meal, as they stood next to the van, Axel peeled the sugar cane and gave each person a chunk.

It was sweet, but mildly so, and it had a stringy texture.

"Do you feel OK, Axel?" Jeff asked. "You don't feel drugged, or anything?"

Axel mimed fainting.

"Ha, ha," sneered Jeff.

They boarded and continued on their way east. They asked Simon to stop again at the Great Rift Valley viewpoint. Lucy bought Jeff a little soapstone figurine of a lion, and he bought her a giraffe.

"We'll always have Magical Giraffe Land," he said.

"Don't say that," said Lucy. "'We'll always have Paris' is how Bogart said goodbye."

"I didn't mean it that way," said Jeff.

"I know you didn't."

It was 5 o'clock sharp when the safari van pulled up to Joe and Helen's house. The safari driver had other customers to pick up, so he left – a normal rental van would carry the team to the airport in two hours.

"Actually," Teddy said, "if we can be ready by 6:30, and if the van is here, we can stop at Uchumi on the way out, in case anyone wants to buy any Kenyan tea or coffee for their partners back home."

The team members took turns showering, changing clothes and repacking.

Jeff, while waiting for his chance to shower, sat on a cheap plastic folding chair in the concrete driveway outside the house. Lucy was in the shower upstairs, Schuyler downstairs. He leaned back slightly and the chair crushed under him.

He apologized profusely and offered to pay for the chair, but Joe laughed it off.

"Those chairs are not well made," he said.

Jeff, however, felt bad about it.

"I came here to help you, not to cost you money. Please, let me give you something."

"Please, don't worry about it," said Joe. Helen had prepared some rice and samosas for the team to eat, and she took Jeff through line and handed him a plate.

"Have something to eat," she said. "You'll feel better."

He did, actually; the samosas were wonderful and the rice was, if bland, filling and comforting. There was a juice drink from an oversized box like the one Jeff had seen made into a wagon in the slums.

Joe came over and put his hand on Jeff's shoulder.

"Jeff, my brother in Christ," he said, "I am glad that you have come here to Kenya."

"Do you think we did anything? Do you think we helped?"

"Of course you helped. The people are excited about making soap, and candles, and the crochet. And we have clean water.

"But the thing you have given us most is hope. You could sit at home back in the U.S. and write a check. Money is an important thing, and I go to the U.S. and I ask for it. But money is not hope. When you come here and give of yourself, you give the people hope."

"God gives them hope," said Jeff. "We are only messengers, and poor ones at that."

"That," said Joe, "is the deeper truth. But I don't think you were a poor messenger."

Jeff smiled and wandered back out onto the driveway with his plate of food. Axel and Kate were already sitting there eating, and Jeff, trying to balance his plate and his glass, sat in the chair next to Kate.

As soon as he did, it broke too.

Jeff's dinner lay in his lap and on his belly as he was sprawled out, crab-like, on the concrete.

All of a sudden, Jeff felt a rush of emotions. He had come here to help, and here he was, a fat American, destroying things.

*How dare he think he could make a difference?*

Axel and Kate helped him clean up the food he had spilled, and the plate he had dropped – he broke that, too. They told him it was nothing, but the blood rushed past his eardrums and he couldn't hear them.

He felt his eyes well up. He didn't want anyone to see him crying, but between the team members, Joe and Helen, and George and Elizabeth (who had stopped by to wish the team a good journey) he couldn't figure out where to go.

He managed to avoid looking at anybody for long enough to finish cleaning up the food and mumble some feeble apology for his clumsiness.

He slipped out the front gate and sat on the curb next to the street.

He started sobbing – great big ridiculous sobs, sobs that might be appropriate if your grandfather had just died but which Jeff knew, even as he cried them, were ridiculous in response to two broken plastic chairs and a plate.

He knew that Axel and Kate would probably come back out onto the driveway once they'd put up the broom and dustpan, so he tried to get the volume under control. His gut knotted up spasmodically, but he thought at least he was quiet enough that they couldn't hear him on the other side of the gate. He choked on his sobs as if they were dry heaves.

*Oh God*, he thought. *Lucy can't see me like this.*

He managed to quell his tears and straighten himself up. He went inside, grabbed some paper towels from the table where the food was laid out, and slipped into the kitchen to moisten them with tap water. He wiped his face and walked into the living room, where Axel, Kate and Teddy were watching American shows on TV.

"You OK, buddy?" asked Axel.

"Yeah, sure," said Jeff.

The team was ready by 6:30, and Pastor Joe had

already called and asked the driver to come early. The team stopped at the Uchumi they had passed on their way to Carnivore. It was a very western-looking supermarket. Several team members bought Kenyan tea or coffee; there was even a brand called "Out of Africa," which reminded Jeff and Lucy of Karen Blixen and her coffee plantation.

Jeff bought a can of Cadbury hot chocolate, which he'd tried one night at George and Elizabeth's.

After Jeff went through the checkout line he stood on the sidewalk in front of the store, waiting for the rest of the team. Lucy emerged and pulled him over to one side.

"So ...." said Lucy.

"Yes?"

"I heard you had a little trouble back at the house."

"I broke a couple of chairs and I felt bad about it."

"And when were you going to tell me?"

"It was nothing."

"It should have been nothing, but I don't think it was nothing. I think you're still beating up on yourself. And you *promised*."

"I didn't want you to see me like that," said Jeff.

"It's been a long trip, Jeff, and we're ready to go home. We're all feeling kind of emotional. There are probably a half a dozen things right now that would start me crying – but I wouldn't really be crying about any of those things. I'd be crying because we're going home and I'm not sure how I feel about that right now. I'm happy and I'm sad and I'm tired and I'm excited and I just really don't know how I feel.

"But if we're going to be together, and if we're going to let each other in, we can't be worried about how we look. I'm not 16, and you're not 16, and there's a romantic part of all this, but if we're going to take it past all of that we can't hide from each other.

"Believe me, Jeff, I know who you are. I know your flaws, or I think I do, and I know the person behind those flaws. And I love that person.

"Don't you dare hide from me now."

He gave her a little peck on the lips.

"I'll do better."

"You'll do fine."

◆

They were at the airport by 8 p.m., two hours before their flight to Amsterdam. Joe and Helen, who had come to the airport in their own car to see the team off and help carry some of the luggage, hugged each of the team members and thanked them again for their efforts.

"You will never know how much God has blessed us through you," said Helen.

The line for check-in was very long and moved very, very slowly.

They finished checking in and then had to stand in the emigration line to have their passports stamped for exit. Then it was upstairs to the departure gate;

they had gone through a metal detector when they first entered the terminal, but there was another security checkpoint at the gate.

Eventually, everyone from the team had passed through security and was seated at the gate. It was crowded, and there was no room for everyone to sit together – and not really enough room for everyone to sit. Jeff stood next to where Lucy was sitting, and looked around the room to find Teddy, and Dea, and Axel, and Kate, and Schuyler.

By 9:30, they were filing onto the plane, and right on time, at five minutes after 10, the plane taxied onto the runway and the Salt+Water ministries team had left Kenya.

On the plane, Jeff sat next to a pair of German tourists who had been on a safari vacation – not at Masai Mara, but at Tsavo West National Park, on the road from Nairobi south to Mombasa. They'd had a sensational time.

After a brief conversation, however, Jeff curled under his blanket and sloped over against the side of the plane. He actually slept this time, for several hours. When he awoke, he watched a movie on the seat-back TV.

He discovered he had to relieve himself. Reluctantly, he disturbed the Germans and they let him out into the aisle. He walked back to the rear of the plane, and noticed Lucy sleeping peacefully a few rows behind his seat. He stopped and looked at her for a second.

"I love you," he whispered.

◆

The plane landed at Schiphol Airport at 6 a.m. They would have an eight-hour layover – "the ultimate anticlimax," as Dea called it – before returning to the U.S. But they planned to kill some time by taking a bus tour of Amsterdam that left from the airport. The ticket booth didn't open until 8, and the first available tour didn't leave until 9:15, so team members had some time to kill. They had breakfast at McDonald's again – five of them, this time, with Teddy and Dea back at the departure gate watching the carry-ons. But then Kate decided she wanted to look at some of the shops again, and she took Lucy along with her.

"How can she look at jewelry after what we've seen this week?" Axel asked.

"Looking isn't the same thing as buying," said Schuyler.

"Well, we're in a place where we have choices about where to go and what to do," said Jeff. "For the past week and a half, we've had to be here and there on somebody else's schedule, and when we did have free time there was nowhere to spend it. So it's fun just to wander around."

"That's right," said Schuyler.

Axel looked at Jeff.

"You've had a pretty good trip, haven't you?"

"I have. And not just because of Lucy.

"Although," he grinned, "Lucy was certainly a part of it."

The bus tour of Amsterdam was great fun. The tour stopped at a windmill that had been turned into a house, and at a wooden shoe factory, where Jeff bought a wheel of Gouda cheese. They drove through the red-light district, where scantily-clad women danced in windows. (Lucy covered Jeff's eyes playfully.)

They drove past the Anne Frank home, where tourists were lined up in the streets to take the tour.

"I wish we could stop and see that," said Dea. "Maybe one of these days."

They marveled at the bicycles everywhere. There was even a downtown parking garage, several levels high, just for bicycles. With help from the tour guide, they translated the euros-per-liter price for gasoline into dollars-per-gallon, and then the use of bicycles wasn't as much of a surprise.

The narrow, narrow townhouses throughout downtown were built during a period of history when taxes were based on street frontage. Each one had a block and tackle hanging over it so that large pieces of furniture could be lifted up from the sidewalk and brought in through an upstairs window.

Later, back at Schiphol, Dea gathered the group together.

"More debrief?" whined Schuyler.

"I just want to say a few words about Amsterdam," Dea said.

"We've just come from a place where the church is growing. We've stopped here in a place where the church has faded away.

"This is a secular place. Not only is it secular, but – and this is partly a separate issue – it's a place where drugs and sex are available more freely than they are even back in the states. And all that makes us as Christians nervous.

"That's another mission trip, and maybe some of you will take that trip one day. But I also want you to notice the things we have to learn from Amsterdam, and from Europe in general. Even on a 90-minute bus trip, seen some of the ways they live more simply, and more efficiently. Their standard of living is similar to ours, but they do it with less consumption. When we think about the poverty we saw last week in Africa, we need to remember Amsterdam, because how we live our lives back in America affects how the world's resources are shared.

"And that's the end of my soapbox. We'll circle up again when we get off the plane in Nashville, and that will be our real closing; I just wanted to talk about Amsterdam while it was still fresh in your mind."

Like Nairobi, the gate at Amsterdam had its own security checkpoint, and so once you had gone through it there was no choice but to sit and wait for boarding.

Jeff sat next to Schuyler. "How are you feeling?"

"I'm OK. I'm just going to go home, and talk to him, and see where we can go from here."

"I'll be praying for you," said Jeff. "I love you, you know that?"

"I know. I love you too, Jeff."

At last, it was time to board the plane for America.

Jeff settled into his seat, stuffed his backpack under the seat in front of him, and looked out the window at the terminal. He felt a tap on his shoulder. It was Lucy.

"Is this seat taken?" she asked.

"I don't have any idea," he said.

"I do. I checked back in Nairobi. They couldn't put me next to you on that flight, but they put me next to you on this one. I hope you don't mind."

Jeff grinned.

Lucy pushed the armrest between them up and out of the way as she sat down and snuggled up next to him.

"God has been good to me," said Jeff.

Jeff began to hear Norah Jones singing love songs, which was funny, because he hadn't plugged in his headset yet.

**END**

## IN REAL LIFE

My own short-term mission experiences have been through LEAMIS International Ministries, a non-denominational group based in Marion County, Tenn. They aren't to be confused with the fictional short-term missions group mentioned in the novel, but I highly recommend them, both for their philosophy and their participant experience.

The words in this volume are my own, however, and LEAMIS (or any other missions organization) is not responsible for them.

More information about LEAMIS can be found at **leamis.org.**

The water purification device mentioned in the novel is also a real device; you can find out more about it at **waterfortheworld.com.**

-- John I. Carney
October, 2008